About the Author

G. Y. Lee is a Hmong anthropologist who was born in Laos but educated in Australia where he has lived for many years with his wife and four children. He is better known among the Hmong as Dr. Lee Yia, and has written widely on his people, their traditions and diaspora. This is his first novel.

A Hmongland Publishing Company Book

www.hmongabc.com

ISBN 0-9723624-0-1

Copyright © 2004 by Hmongland Publishing Company

Printed and manufactured in the United States of America

Cover artwork by Kia Vang

Design by Xai Xiong

Please address all inquiries and feedback to hmongabc@hmongabc.com.

Preface

This story is based on real events that took place at one particular juncture in the history of Hmong refugees from Laos when Ban Vinai was used as a refugee camp for them in Thailand from 1975 to 1992.

Although many of the people found in the story actually existed, their names have been changed where they have direct relation to the events that are told here. I have also changed the countries and cities where the people, on whom the main characters are based, now live. The lead protagonist, Mua, referred to in the first person in the story should not be taken to be the author; he is only a fictitious character.

This is an attempt to use fiction to depict the way of life in historical context of two different groups of people, the Hmong and Thai. One is spontaneous and giving, living from moment to moment and not worrying much about tomorrow. The other is cautious and reticent, clinging to some firmly held beliefs — sometimes at great personal cost. It is hoped that cultural understanding will be made more vivid through this creative process.

I would like to thank Yuepheng Xiong of Hmong ABC, whose faith in the book has seen its publication, and Xai Xiong for his beautiful cover design and help with the text. Permission to use the painting of the Hmong girl by Ms. Kia Vang, one of our very talented Hmong artists, on the front cover is here gratefully acknowledged. My thanks also go to my wife Maylee Lee for her ideas and support, as well as the following friends and colleagues for their comments on the original draft: Peggy Heng, Linda Pettersson, Maria Caraglio, Pauline Franks, Warren Duncan, Frieda de Jong, Dr. Kaoly Yang, Thongrith Phoumirath, Dr. Pao and Natrudy Saykao and Kaying Yang who not only made many beautiful suggestions but also proved to be a great inspiration.

— G. Y. Lee

DUST OF LIFE

A TRUE BAN VINAI LOVE STORY

G. Y. Lee

Chapter 1

"In a way, she is related to you, Mua," my mother said to me.

"Really? But do I know her?" I asked.

"You know her mother and father. Her name is Pafua."

"That's a nice name, Flower of the Clouds," I mused to myself.

This young Hmong girl was among the first things my mother told me as we were discussing the refugees who escaped from Laos to seek asylum in 1975 in Thailand. My mother, three brothers and their families had earlier been accepted to resettle in the United States and had just arrived in March 1976 in Minneapolis, Minnesota, where I was living. I had not seen them for more than five years since taking up my university studies there.

During the first few weeks after her arrival, my mother spent much of her time talking about the harrowing suffering she and other Hmong went through during their escape from the new communist regime in Laos, and the hardship they had to put up with in overcrowded Thai refugee camps. As Thailand would only give them temporary stay with the support of the Office of the United Nations High Commission for Refugees, most of the political asylum seekers needed to apply for permanent settlement in a third country. France, Canada, America and Australia had been the main countries interested in accepting them. Pafua and her family wanted to come and live in America, but could not find a sponsor.

My mother then proceeded to tell me about her and her parents, who they were and how we were related to each other. Her mother was a distant cousin to my father so I did know them, although I had not met her daughter in person but had heard of her on previous occasions.

"What does she want me to do?" I asked my mother.

"Read the letter and look at her photo," my mother said. "If you like her, see what you can do to help her and her family. They really want to come here and need your help. Her step-father has other wives and is no longer with them. Her mother has a brother in Australia but they don't want to go there."

"Why is that? He could help get them to go and live with him," I observed.

"Yes, but there are so few Hmong in Australia. It will be a very lonely life there."

We were sitting in the kitchen of our rented house on Greenwood Avenue. My mother went through one of her over-flowing bags and took out an envelop which she handed to me. They had met in the refugee camp in Ban Vinai, and Pafua had given her a letter and her photo to bring to me to see if I would be interested in sponsoring her. I took a glance at the passport-size black and white photo. Pafua had a long angular face, long black hair and a small nose. Her eyes showed signs of kindness like someone who was responsible and mature. I was quite taken by her appearance and her appeal for my assistance.

"You know, mother, the only way I can sponsor her family is if I am married to Pafua or if I am closely related to her by birth. But I am neither. Also, I already have a girlfriend. I haven't told you about her. We have known each other for almost two years. She lives in Washington, D.C., with her uncle," I said teasingly to my mother to see how she would react.

"Well, who is she, this girlfriend of yours? Is she a Hmong girl?" she asked, suddenly interested.

"No, she is Lao but she is very nice. I got to know her through the Lao Students Association. Her uncle was the previous Ambassador to the US for the old Royal Lao government. They are now refugees here, just like us."

"That sounds too high for you, son. She is like the ray of light from the sky and you are like the blade of grass on the ground," my mother reflected on our difference in social status.

"Mother, these days people don't think like that anymore, especially in America. We are supposed to be all equal here. I have a master's degree and she only finished a receptionist course from a vocational college. That would make us even, don't you think?" I joked.

"I still don't like it. You'll be better off with a Hmong wife. Pafua would suit you better. She is a very capable girl. She has no father, as you know. She only has her mother, a younger brother and sister. But she takes care of them well. Few young people can do that. I know you'll like her when you see her," my mother said, trying hard to convince me.

"What will I do with Damdouan, my Lao girlfriend?"

"She'll be alright. She's lucky she is already in America. She's not like Pafua who is stuck in a refugee camp in Thailand with no money, no future and nowhere to go. Besides, you will do her and her family a good turn and she will always love you for it," my strong-willed mother replied as if she knew that would be the best thing for me.

"Well, I can't promise anything, but I'll think about it and let you know," I said.

"Yes. I don't think you can be wrong," she persisted, almost as if she was handing me her decision on the matter.

Pafua, this young Hmong girl, I remember her well from that summer long ago when I first saw her in the childhood of my memories. That year when I came to know of her, we lived in a mud house at the top of some wet rice fields, below two other mud houses that belonged to my cousins. The houses were simple rectangular structures with walls made from dried mud suspended on bamboo frames and covered in thatched grass tied down to timber trusses. The floor of the house was made only of simple compacted dirt. Beyond the houses lie the open fields that were drying under the hot sun of the summer days, and lower down was the stream that flowed past the fields into a bigger river a few miles down where the southern end of the town finished. In the dry season, the river ran low and clear, meandering through many other rice terraces with pebbles of different colors along the river banks left there by the flood during the monsoon season when the river overflowed and transformed into a torrent of mud. Beyond the fields were small rolling hills where water buffaloes roamed in search of fresh grass to eat and water to drink and to wade in to cool down the summer heat beating down on their backs. Most of the hills had no trees but were covered in grass; a few of them were lined with deep trenches cutting across the slopes near the top that were used by soldiers of times past in their front line defense of the town through the centuries.

During its lifetime, the town had changed hands many times between Vietnamese, Thai, Lao and French colonizers, showing thus a rich mixture of architecture that stood the test of time and testified to this crossing of cultures. The Buddhist temples were big and distinctly Lao, their yellow golden roofs shining in the hot sun. The brick buildings, used by people who worked for the government, were in the French style with their rustic tiled roofs and dust-covered cement-rendered walls. Some of the walls had been chipped from being hit by gunfire during battles between anti-colonial Vietnamese troops and French soldiers who fought for control of Indochina in the years before the mid-1950's.

As a small country in the throes of independence from French colonial control at the time, Laos was nestled between Thailand to the west, China to the north, Vietnam to the east and Cambodia to the south. Laos had no sea access and was surrounded by neighbors who were more aggressive and powerful. In the 1960's, its population was reported to number about three million people. Throughout its long history, it was forever drawn into war with one of these neighboring nations or between factions within its borders who aligned themselves with these countries' political ambitions. The French first went into Laos to help advise the King of Luang Prabang on what to do against armed incursions into the country by the Thai, but took over the country as a protectorate in 1883. They also controlled Vietnam and Cambodia, making the three neighboring countries into a single colony called French Indochina. French colonial authorities ran the colony from Vietnam with Vietnamese as local civilian staff and lower ranking army officers. Following the second World War, Ho Chi Minh was building his anti-French movement in North Vietnam with Japanese assistance and attracted the interest of local nationalists in Laos, some of whom went there to join him and to get support for their own struggle for independence. The Soviet Union was soon drawn into the conflict when it agreed to help Ho Chi Minh and his Vietminh troops in their fight against French domination.

In the mid-1950's, the Pathet Lao (Lao Homeland) revolutionary movement in Laos sided with the Soviet-supported Vietminh in North Vietnam. As opposition to this, the Royal Lao government was set up with the support of the French government and was putting up armed resistance against the North Vietnamese and the Pathet Lao. After the French withdrew from the region in 1954, the United States became increasingly involved, and a see-saw war soon developed back and forth along the Lao-Vietnamese border, with Muang Khun located directly in its path. Vietnam was by this time divided into North and South Vietnam, with the North under the influence of China and the Soviet Union, and the South aligned with the free world and America. The big battles between the two sides were conducted in Vietnam, but many smaller ones also took place in Cambodia and Laos with their own winners and losers, although little was known to the outside world about them then. The Hmong as a hill minority in the northern part of the country were recruited into the factions involved in these armed conflicts, and sometimes brothers found themselves fighting on different sides of the Lao political divide. For many centuries, they fought against Chinese control of their territories in southern China until they were overpowered and had to flee south to Vietnam, Laos and Thailand. And now even here, the same armed struggles continued with their predictable tragic results.

The town and Pafua's family were part of these surroundings in this early period of my life. I saw her for the first time that summer of 1958. Or more to the point, I saw her being carried by her mother as an unborn child. I remember her mother and father well. They were very important people during those years in the 1950's in the outback town of Muang Khun in northern Laos, where I was finishing primary school. As I walked past her father's house to and from school, I would often see his two wives or children in and around the main two-story house, or doing things at the smaller out-house which was used as the family's kitchen and dining area. The smaller house was built by my father and we used to live there until 1955 when her father took it over from us. The older of the two wives was related to my mother, and they often stopped and chatted with each other in the middle of whatever they were doing or wherever they were going.

Pafua's father was a commanding provincial police officer in 1957, one of the few people of an ethnic minority to be in such positions at the time. One day in 1958, we heard that he had married a third wife and it turned out to be her mother. She was the sister of a very prominent Hmong leader who once was the director-general of the Ministry of Education in Laos in the 1960's. I had never seen her mother before, but she was a very beautiful woman with very fair skin, the mark of a person used to a gentle and well-to-do life. She was still young, maybe in her early thirties, although she was married before to a Hmong soldier in the Lao Army who was the brother of a famous chief in Nong Het, in northeastern Laos. Her mother's first husband had died in a battle at the front line a few years earlier somewhere in Pak Kha, a stronghold of communist rebels who were opposing the Royal Lao government and its Western allies.

I used to see her mother and the other wives, with some of their children or servants taking walks on the grounds of their large compound which was surrounded by thick bamboo trees used as a sort of fence and boundaries on all four sides. It was about three or four acres in a square shape, like the many surrounding residential blocks aligning the rubble road that were developed by the French for their colonial service officers before their permanent return to France. Only the blocks of land were left because all the brick houses had been destroyed by bombs during the battle with the Vietminh from North Vietnam in 1953. In 1959, her father was killed in an ambush with a number of other Hmong officials on their way to negotiate peace with rebel troops in Nong Het. It took them a few days to recover the bodies. They held a big funeral for her father in the small out-house, and buried him somewhere far north of the city. At that time, rumors of an impending civil war never stopped at Muang Khun, and no one paid very much attention to what happened to other people's lives so I cannot remember when exactly Pafua was born. In any case, it must be difficult to be born without knowing one's father. Not long after, we heard that her mother remarried and moved to live in the new husband's village.

Every few weeks, we saw government troops dressed in green battle fatigues walking in single columns under the weight of their big back packs and heavy guns along the main road of the town towards the Vietnamese border. Our teachers told us that they were going "to chase after the enemy," but we never saw them return. Sometimes in the middle of a lesson, someone would come and tell us to leave class because the war was said to have come to the town that minute, and everyone would run home, scared and all out of breath. But, of course, it would turn out to be just a false alarm and we would return to school the next day.

Then in January 1961, the war did finally come. The schools were closed for good, and the people went hiding in different directions. Some returned to the town and started life again under a new regime, a new faction of the war. My family kept on the run because my father was serving on the losing side, the side supported by the Americans. After leaving in 1961, we never saw the town of Muang Khun again. It had been reduced to rubble in the many battles to regain its control that followed. Finally, on the order of the Military Regional Commander of the Royal Lao government and aided by heavy artillery guns fired by Hmong ground troops from the surrounding hills, the US Air Force pounded the old city out of existence from the safety of their high-flying jet bombers in order to deprive the Pathet Lao of its occupation in April 1969. Since then, the new Lao government did not have enough money to rebuild it from its ashes, and decided not to even name it in the new maps of the country. Now only a cluster of villages consisting of grass houses and make-shift temples stand in place of the old French colonial two-story brick buildings and former century-old shining Buddhist stupas.

Although I was born to Hmong parents, I never really had a typical Hmong life with all its cultural fineries. After I was about two years of age, my father enlisted in the French colonial army and my parents went to live in Muang Khun which only had a small number of Hmong families scattered in various parts of the town. Most of its population were Lao, with a few Chinese and Vietnamese shop-keepers. There might be the occasional funerals and the New Year celebrations which provided me with the chance to see Hmong customs, but that hardly made me well informed about them. After the war came to Muang Khun in 1961, I left my family in various refugee camps in Xieng Khouang and spent my time in Vientiane, the capital of Laos, where I pursued my education, staying with Lao families and in a boarding school run by French officials. I studied foreign ideas and languages, like other young people at the time who found themselves living in a country with many minorities dominated by French colonial masters. Although I could speak the Hmong language, I was not interested in other aspects of the Hmong culture. Instead, I reveled in Western books and dabbled in Western cultural traditions, firmly believing them to be the ideal directives in life.

Because of this, it was like a dream come true when I finally went in 1967 to Minneapolis, Minnesota, in the United States for my university studies after I obtained a government scholarship. I left Laos while my father was stationed with other troops in the far north of the country defending the border against communist incursions. We did not even see each other to say good-bye. I gradually lost touch with people I used to know in my childhood. Old friends and acquaintances went their separate ways and were too busy making ends meet in the midst of the Lao civil war. New battles and new victories or losses kept us on different sides, stranded in different places or forever in search of a peaceful enclave to stay alive. Not long after I went to America, my father died in a battle in Laos. It was too far for me to come to the funeral and I never really had the chance to farewell him properly — in life or in death.

By the end of 1974, I had completed both my bachelor's and master's degrees in agriculture at Minnesota, seven years after leaving Laos. In early 1975, I was doing odd jobs waiting for my university graduation when the revolutionary war ended with the communists gaining control of Indochina, of which Laos used to be an integral part. Before I could return home, my mother and brothers had escaped with the first wave of Hmong refugees from Laos to Thailand in that year. The Hmong on the Royal Lao government side were serving in the so-called secret army supported by the American Central Intelligence Agency in the 1960's and were strongly opposed to the new regime which also did not look kindly upon them now that it was in power. No one wanted to stay under the new communist authorities. Twenty thousand refugees crossed the

Mekong River to Thailand during the first three months after the Pathet Lao take-over in April 1975. By the following year, more than 80,000 Hmong were living in three refugee camps in Thailand along the border with Laos at Nam Yao, Loei and Nong Khai. During the early 1980's, this number swelled to more than 120,000 people, and the United Nations High Commission for Refugees had to set up a fourth refugee camp in Chiangkham, Payao Province. Those Hmong who could not escape to Thailand fled to hide in the remote jungles of Xieng Khouang Province and other parts of northeastern Laos, still putting up armed resistance against the new rulers to this very day.

For these reasons, I decided that I had no choice but to remain in America and, if possible, to see how I could get my relatives to come and live with me from the Thai refugee camp. After receiving my master's degree in agricultural development from the University of Minnesota, one of my professors, who was a well-known development anthropologist, asked me if I wanted to go to Thailand to work for a year with one of the Thai government's tribal development projects in Chiangmai. He had been interested in highland development in northern Thailand for many years and was completing a book on the Hmong there at the time. At my request, he had also visited my family and other refugees in Thai refugee camps in August 1975 and helped to apply for them to join me in America. Due to his strong urging and assistance, I obtained an exchange fellowship from one of the local American foundations and was getting ready to go to Thailand when much to my joy, my mother, brothers and their families arrived to start their new life with me.

Chapter 2

Minnesota, the State of Ten Thousand Lakes, is in the midwest of the United States just south of Canada, sandwiched between Wisconsin to the east, Iowa to the south, and North and South Dakota to the west. It was very cold in winter with snow covering the ground from November to early April each year. Spring, just after the melting of the snow, was the most beautiful season when nature suddenly returned to life with everything becoming green, grass shooting up from muddy patches of dirt and trees budding into young leaves flickering in the breeze. The lakes, with the snow gone, came back to being filled with clear water instead of ice and snow, making you feel that once again everything around you was given a fresh breath of air from nature and was now adorned with life, the wild flowers showing their abundance among the grass. Like the green leaves on the trees, people started to come out and enjoy the open air in big numbers, unlike during the winter months. Nature had returned and everything now became normal again.

I had been renting student accommodation at the University, and had to find larger housing for my mother, brothers and their families. I could not find anything affordable in Minneapolis, but was able to get something cheaper in one of the more run-down streets near University Avenue in St. Paul, its twin city. It was not as noisy as University Avenue, but still had some traffic going through most of the day. Many of the houses were built with timber and old, but were well insulated from the winter cold and had good heating. We were surrounded by many other poor people of all ethnicities, but did not feel unsafe living with them. We were too busy settling in and did not have time to be concerned. There were talks about young people forming gangs which sometimes terrorized the neighborhood, but we did not really see any of them.

We were among the first Hmong refugees from Laos to settle in Minnesota, and received a lot of help from the local Catholic Refugee Service, although we were not Catholic ourselves. At the time, other

Hmong refugees had just started to arrive from refugee camps in Thailand, sponsored mainly by American church groups in small cities and rural communities. Some converted to Christianity because of this early link, but most later migrated to Minneapolis-St. Paul where they could find employment, better help and services. I continued to stay at the University and only visited my mother and brothers on weekends. The week my mother arrived, the snow had started to melt, but there were still large patches of it in many places and it was really cold when the wind blew. My mother was not used to such icy weather and complained bitterly about my choice of residence. She said that she would prefer to be in another state where it was warmer and where you could walk around safely without falling on your back along the snow-covered slippery footpaths and risked breaking your hips and bones.

After my mother had told me about Pafua, I did a lot of thinking during the next few days to see if and how I could help her. Her plight in the refugee camp and her courage in sending for me, an almost complete stranger, made me really feel for her. But because she was not part of my immediate family, it would be easier for me to apply for her and her family to resettle in the US if she was to become my wife. This was what she was suggesting in her letter "but only if we like each other," she wrote. I was flattered by this request that showed a lot of daring on her part. The child I saw her mother carrying had become a young woman and now wanted my help. I was thinking that perhaps this would be my chance to be a white knight in shining armor, going forth to rescue a maiden in distress. After a few days of consideration, I wrote back to her in the refugee camp. Two weeks later, she replied that she had gone to Bangkok to study English while waiting to see which Western country she should apply for resettlement. Not knowing each other well, we wrote only short letters with little to say to each other in those early days that marked the beginning of our hesitant relationship.

One day, Pafua wrote to me that she had gone to Oudontani, a provincial city in northeastern Thailand. She wanted to study dressmaking to make a living in the refugee camp. She did not ask me to send her money, but she told me about how much her living expenses and study fees were. By then, we had assumed that we would be friends and I would eventually get her to America. I sent her $500 which was a lot of money for me as a recently graduated student. She soon wrote back to thank me. That was the first time I sent money to her, and I was pleased to do it as it showed that she now knew me enough to want to accept things from me. It also made me happy to be able to help her and her family. I felt as if we were already close to each other, as if we were meant to be together eventually in the not-too-distant future.

We continued to write — about ourselves, what we did and what we felt about various things. Sometimes, I would try to imagine what she would be like in real life when I would finally see her in person. Would she look young but serious like in her photo, or older but still lively and high-spirited? If she came to America, what kinds of clothes would she prefer, traditional Lao costumes or modern European fashion? Would she put on perfume and smell like one of those American girls I passed in the corridor of the big supermarket near the University? I could not wait to know. I read many articles on Thailand and rural development, and presented a few papers at my department at the University. At the end of 1976, my exchange fellowship came through and I was ready to go and work in Thailand, as arranged by my professor. I wrote to Pafua and said I was coming. It took her a while to reply, but she said that she was looking forward to our first meeting and that I should go to see her after my arrival in the country. I was anxious to get to know her in person to see if I could help her as she had hoped, and perhaps we could marry if we got along or were attracted to each other.

I also wrote to Damdouan, my Lao friend in Washington D.C., to say that I was going to work for a year in Thailand and would write to her when I got there. I did not want to talk to her by telephone; I was afraid to hear her voice. Although she had been keeping in touch with me through phone calls and the occasional letters, she had not always been on my mind, but our relationship could become better if I took more time to focus on it. Until now, she seemed to be the one more interested to carry on beyond more than friendship. Although I told my mother that Damdouan was my girlfriend, I had kept her at arms length, as I really did not know how her uncle would treat a hill tribe young man like me. I had met him a few times, and he seemed to be a very dignified and friendly man. I really did not know if he would look down on my background like some other high class lowland people in Laos. For now, I was more concerned to see how things would go with Pafua first, because she was the one who needed my help the most.

After a few weeks of preparation, I left for Thailand and I arrived in Bangkok in September 1976. It was in the middle of the summer. The weather was very hot and humid, with frequent rains pouring down on the big city that never seemed to go to sleep with people strolling along many of the main streets looking at the night stalls that sprang up along the sidewalks. Cars, trucks, buses and motor cycles filled the roads most times of the day seemingly without following much of the local traffic rules, competing against each other to see which ones would be able to squeeze past the others without causing an accident or denting its neighbors. After a few days in Bangkok to get my immigration clearance, I went on to Chiangmai. I was to be placed with the Tribal Development Center (TDC), operated by the Thai Ministry of Welfare on the grounds of Chiangmai University where I would be given a Thai counterpart worker to train. That was the arrangement made by my American professor who had a lot to do with setting up the Center. The Center's director, Khun Somboon, was also pleased that I was going to be the first Hmong to work with them, and he was eager to see what contribution I could make to his institution. On my part, I was keen to see what the Center had been doing with the local hill tribe villagers and with what results.

Chapter 3

The first night I arrived by air-conditioned bus in Chiangmai, I met Khun Samanh who was a tricycle or "samlo" driver. He was stationed outside the entrance to the hotel where the bus I travelled on from Bangkok terminated. Seeing me getting out of the bus with my luggage, he lunged forward and asked where I would be staying and if I wanted to "have fun." He had a dark complexion with rather short hair, and wore cotton Thai peasant outfits like most "samlo" drivers — blue shorts matched with a blue short-sleeved shirt without neck. I had kept up my Thai language through a lot of reading while in America and I was able to speak Thai quite well. I said to him that I was tired after a day on the bus and only wanted to rest. The street was full of cars, buses, taxis and tricycles. The traffic in front of the hotel was heavy and noisy. Pollution was hanging in the open hot air like angry spirits demanding to be relieved with food and drinks, making your face and arms itchy as a reminder. All I wanted was to find a quiet room to get away from the polluting air and the ear-splitting traffic, and have a good sleep for the night. I told him so, but he said that would be no problem, as he could get some nice young lady to come up to my room and help massage my pain away.

I had this approach used on me at the hotel in Bangkok before, so I continued to say "no." I got a room and took the lift up. In the lift, the hotel porter also asked if I wanted a good time. I was beginning to wonder whether the female body was the only thing that pre-occupied people in Thailand. After having my shower, I heard a knock on the door and went to investigate. Khun Samanh and a young Thai woman were standing there, beaming at me. I told him that I already said I did not want to be disturbed. He just kept smiling at me, while the woman was fidgeting in embarrassment, a large white handbag hanging from her left shoulder. She was rather tall with long hair and a pink shirt tucked into a pair of white slacks. Her body was very nicely proportioned and beautiful, but she had put on too much make-up and looked almost like a Cantonese opera singer you see lamenting some fateful story line in a Chinese movie from Hong Kong or Taiwan.

Not wanting other guests to see us arguing at the door, I asked them to come inside my room. Samanh introduced the young woman as Virachit, and told me that she would help me relax as she was his "best girl." He made it sound as if he had selected her especially for me. She looked vulnerable, just standing there and not saying a word, as if she was waiting for a sentence to be handed down at a trial on her livelihood. I had not been with professional Thai ladies before, and I was rather embarrassed but I could never say "no" to anyone for long like the rain that could not help falling when darkening clouds appear in the sky. Samanh told me to just enjoy my visit to Chiangmai and "don't think too much" (*mai tong kheet mak*). Maybe, like me, he believed that life was full of mysteries with many unexpected twists and turns so that you should enjoy the daffodils along the trail in front of you rather than wait to find the deceptive perfume of the unseen red rose whose thorns could cause deep cuts to your unprotected fingers. He left the woman in the room and said he would come back for her tomorrow. Then, just as quickly he disappeared out the door.

I knew I was going to have to pay for this service which I did not request. But I did not want to subject Virachit to further rejection and embarrassment, so I invited her to sit down on one of the twin beds in the room. She asked me to call her "Chit for short, please," and said she would like to take a shower, and proceeded into the bathroom with her hand bag. After a few minutes, she came out in a short cream dressing gown and I realized that she was very fair-skinned, not like other Thai women I had seen. She told me that she was a northern Thai, and most northern Thai women were rather fair in comparison to their sisters in other parts of the country. As she sat on the bed and started to take off her gown, I noticed that without any vestige of clothing, she was blessed with a body to-die-for. She had a rather slender frame, but what stood out about her was her chest — adorned with a pair of pointed breasts. They were full and round and were not sagging as if to announce with pride that their owner was in the prime of her young life and ready for any challenges. God really knows how to make women a thing of great beauty and an enticement to men's eyes and senses! They are like the daisies that colour the meadow and scent it with fragrance in the early morning so that buffaloes will be drawn to the green grass, and men will be moved to work hard toiling at the earth, bringing out the songs of love, the good feelings and the admiration of all things beautiful that give them the strength to go forth in life.

Except for a small scar on her left knee, her skin was unblemished and white, almost like that of those beautiful European movie stars men often fantasized about. I was sure that my jaw must have dropped and my mouth open looking at that living object of splendor in front of me. She was soon wrapping herself with a light blue towel she picked up from a rack at the end of the hotel bed, as if to say that I should do something or I would be denied the pleasure of the occasion. I was sorry to see that splendid sight disappear from view. In a matter of seconds, all my shyness disappeared and I did not know how, but so did my forlorn clothes. I was too excited to talk, so without a word I pulled her down on the bed and went to work. In those days, there was no talk about safe sex. I had all but forgotten about catching diseases from her, and even if I did I would not have cared at that moment when all I could think of was to enjoy that soft and full body and those superb breasts for all my money's worth. I still did not know how much the experience would cost me, but it did not seem to matter at all then.

She felt warm and smelled like ripe pawpaws being opened for dessert at a romantic picnic under the cool shade of an expansive bodhi tree. I could not believe that a young woman with such a body would want to share it with so many men for money, but then I probably would have done the same if I was her. Why waste it on one man? She was soon putting on a show of sighing and thrashing at me, her eyes closed and her face contorted with pleasure. Her huge white melons were swinging up and down her small chest — smooth and silky yet just an illusion afterwards like the white mist surrounding the mountain tops around Hmong villages in the morning. The whimpering sound of her moaning and heavy breathing were like the lush flute music floating through romance films playing in the big movie houses with their clear and expensive stereo sound systems. She seemed oblivious to everything around us, abandoning herself to her pleasure and the task at hand, as if she was really enjoying it and it was not just another paying customer doing the same routine act she had to put up with many times a day.

As we sat on the bed afterwards, tired but happy, I ordered two bottles of Coke from room service and gave her one. I asked her how old she was and where she came from. She said she was twenty three and came from Maerim, east of Chiangmai city.

"I suppose you don't like people asking you these personal questions?" I asked her.

"No, I don't mind people asking me. Not many of the customers are interested in who I am and where I came from. They just want to enjoy my body, pay for it and let me go. It's just like buying something at a shop."

"Really! But there must be some feeling or some attraction? How can you do it otherwise?"

"You've got two choices: just pretend you really enjoy it or you're not there and let them do what they want with you," she explained.

"So what you did with me just now was pretending you really enjoyed it?"

"Well, in a sort of way I did really enjoy myself. I don't know why. You looked shy and fresh, and it was like a new leaf for me after the regular old men and tourists in this town. Most men want to think they're the best or the most attractive in bed. You have to play along with the game. But sometimes, I do really enjoy myself as well. With certain men, that is. There is an old white-haired man who lives here and comes two or three times a week to see me. Even though he is old, he is really good. But I prefer younger men."

"It's good that you can enjoy yourself as well. But you still haven't told me how you got into this line of work," I said, looking at her and wishing I could keep her magnificent bosom with me so I could put it on a shrine as a supreme object of art for my worship and admiration.

Later after we had discussed many little things about Thailand and she became less shy, Chit told me that she used to be married to a policeman who slept around and gave her the clap so that she had to have a hysterectomy and now could no longer have children, about her divorce from her useless husband and her being unable to find employment to support herself. I found her life story so sad I just did not feel like doing anything more with her the rest of that night. We had all but forgotten about the massage that was supposed to be the reason Samanh sent her to me in the first place. We slept in separate beds. The next morning she told me that Samanh was really a very nice and helpful person and that he would do anything for anyone, even at great cost to himself. She said he was very kind to her and gave her a lot of business for a commission. His tricycle driving was a way for him to get customers for some of the big operators in the business, she said. I paid her 200 Baht and she eagerly exited out the door, like a prisoner happy to be released from her cell for some fresh air and a more normal life outside.

At the beginning, I was rather shocked by the casual attitude many people in Thailand had towards the paid sex industry. Wherever I went at that time, I seemed to come across these ladies of the night. The oldest profession appeared to be everywhere — just like a normal job giving people a living, and its followers seemed to enjoy doing their work and did not appear to be treated like trashy aliens from another planet. I was impressed by the open-mindedness and generosity of these people who appeared to take things easy and to be contented with their lives from one day to the next. They might not have something to eat tomorrow, but it did not seem to bother them because they could rely on help from others around them. As Buddhist, they believed in giving and being kind, so that you would accumulate merits and be born as a better person or a higher being in the next life. Like what some high-brow American academics were saying, maybe the poor people and the peasantry in this world have got their own noble morality to live by, despite and because of the harsh way in which life often deals with them.

I did not think too much of the incident with Chit, although I went over her life story in my head most of the next day. I was also hoping that I would not meet only girls like Chit while I was in Thailand. I did not know then that this first experience and other subsequent encounters with members of the Thai opposite sex would profoundly change the destiny of the Hmong girl I had come to Thailand to rescue.

Chapter 4

To go to the TDC, I took a "songtaeo" or a pick-up utility taxi with a roof over its tray and two rows of seats on the inside of the tray. As I rode in the taxi with other passengers, I noticed how busy Chiangmai city could be in the early morning with many people driving to work. Taxis were also ferrying people to various places and markets, carrying heavy loads on their roofs with drivers beeping loudly on their horns to attract passengers or calling out the directions they were heading. The markets we passed were full of people, shoppers as well as sellers peddling their goods on the grounds or on tables set up in rows inside the market area. It was a really busy, lively and noisy city. People and cars seemed to be going every which direction, as if there was little or no traffic rules to follow. This seemed a real contrast to American city traffic where you could see a lot of people and cars, but would hear few car horns or sounds from commuters who seldom talked to each other and the only noise was from cars, buses or trains whistling their ways to their destinations.

Khun Somboon, the TDC director, met me in his office which was on the first floor of the Center. Apart from a meeting room and the staff work area, there was also a library with many books and reports in both Thai and English for use by the Center staff and by visitors. Many students from Chiangmai University and even foreign researchers were often found browsing through the library shelves. Khun Somboon discussed with me his work plan for me and his trainee worker, my counterpart who was away on a field trip to the hills that day. Khun Somboon was a kindly tall man, and dark like most Thai from central Thailand. He spoke with a loud voice, although at times he sounded more like a father than a strict manager. After a few minutes of meeting, I knew that we were not going to get on well because he did not seem to be able to listen, never asked for his subordinates' opinions, and he kept calling the Hmong by the name many of them intensely disliked: Meo.

This has continued all these years to be the position of the Center and hence the Thai government, even when the preferred term "Hmong" has long been adopted world-wide. His condescending attitude rather put me off.

The TDC was the only government facility advising the Thai government on hill tribe needs and problems, but it had no staff of tribal background at that time. All the 15 or so staff members were from Thai or some other lowland ethnic groups. I was introduced to them by Khun Somboon who asked one of them to go with me later that day to collect my luggage from the hotel and to help find me a cheaper boarding house near the Maeping River to stay for a few weeks while they tried to find me a Hmong settlement with a suitable project for me to be involved in. I spent the next three days looking at a few Hmong villages around Chiangmai to get to know better how the Hmong were living. These villages only had a few households in them and were not taking part in any opium growing or development projects which I would like to study to see if the huge amounts of foreign aid spent on them had done anything for the living standards of the Hmong in the cold highlands of Thailand.

This was the first time I had set foot in real Hmong villages for many years. The only other times were when I was in primary school nearly 20 years before during a visit my mother made with me to relatives near Muang Khun. Seeing Hmong in their villages brought back many childhood memories, making me feel as if I was back in my old country when it was still peaceful and we could go to any place any time. But the Hmong houses in Thailand were rather different from the ones I saw in my childhood in Laos. Here, some of the houses were covered with corrugated iron roofing material and others in thatched grass, while in Laos they were nearly all built with timber walls and covered with wooden shingles. Other than this, the houses were all rectangle in their design. Around the villages, one could hear cicadas singing in the middle of the day, and the sound of roosters crowing from their scavenging patches in the nearby bushes. As most of the adult residents were out in the fields, there was little human movement in the villages during the day, and all seemed to be sleepy and quiet.

On the fourth day, the TDC director asked me to go to a Hmong village called Pakia in Ampher Chiangdao, east of Chiangmai city. He wanted me to find out what the Hmong there needed from the Thai government and to write a report for him. I was given a lift to the village in an old Land Rover driven by one of the extension workers attached to the TDC. He was a young man in his early twenties, still single and a recent graduate in agriculture from one of the universities in the south of the country. I did not know what he was doing at the Hmong village where the Thai-Australian Highland project was conducting crop and cattle-grazing experiments to see how the economy and farming practices of the hill tribes could be improved. A whole contingent of assorted Thai and foreign agricultural experts were stationed there in their own well-built quarters a few kilometers up the hill from the Hmong village. From my discussion with the villagers, it did not look like the two groups had much to do with each other.

The Hmong at Pakia, mostly of the Green Hmong sub-group, were living in two clusters. The smaller village, at the top of the hill next to the Thai-Australian Highland project had only four families which were all related to each other. Nhang Xo, the head of the group, told me that they were of the Zhang clan. This was the name used by Green Hmong but this clan name changed to Lee in the White Hmong dialect. For that reason, he said that being a White Hmong from the Lee clan, I was related to them by the sharing of a common clan name, and he insisted that I stay the night in his house.

"This is your house and we are your family. Don't go to the house of strangers," he said, referring to Hmong of other clans in the village.

I was very touched by his hospitality. He seemed happy and proud that there was an educated Hmong like me working with the Thai authorities when hardly any Hmong in Thailand at that time was literate and educated.

About one kilometer down a steep slope was the bigger settlement with its houses scattered along the top of a small ridge overlooking a deep valley below. Most of the hills around the village were covered in elephant grass from years of slash and burn cultivation, with only a few clumps of trees left here and there where it was too steep to clear for farming. Many kinds of crops were grown here in small clearings, but no opium cultivation could be seen. Domestic animals like dogs, chickens and pigs roamed freely in and around the settlement between the timber houses and the small gardens in their backyards.

After our arrival at the bigger settlement, I talked to a few elderly men and women who stayed home to mind the children while the rest of their families were out tending to the household crops. Later in the evening, I went to see Zong Tu, the headman, and other Hmong after their return from the fields. Like many of the village people, they told me that their biggest need was land for farming, as the Thai Forestry Department was moving into the highlands with hundreds of laborers to plant trees in areas traditionally used for agriculture by the hill tribes. He was concerned that this would displace the villagers from their present location once they ran out of land to farm. They also told me that they would like the government to construct roads to their rice fields so that they could transport their rice harvest home. At the time, they were using either horses or their own backs to do this since many of them had no horses for this work. I did not say anything but I was thinking that this was a rather tall order to ask, building roads to Hmong rice fields scattered on steep mountains over a wide area. These government projects really had given the villagers high hopes that were not going to be fulfilled, but they did not know this.

I spent the night in Nhang Xo's house in the smaller village up the hill near the project site. After dinner, we talked well into the night, sitting around the smoky fireplace. He asked me things about America and I, in turn, asked him about Hmong life and customs. Although there was bright electrical lighting at the project station, the Hmong village had no such luxury and was in darkness, its residents having to rely on candles or kerosene lamps to see at night. The women were finishing off the day's chores; the younger girls gave the dirt house floor a last sweep with a grass broom while the older ones attended to their neglected embroideries in front of the flickering candle light while sharing a quiet conversation together. It was about one o'clock in the morning before we decided to turn in. We did not sleep very long. It seemed that sleep had only just caught up with me when I awoke to the noise of my host's wife going about the early morning's household work as roosters made their first crows outside. With the help of the eldest daughter, they lit the fire, fetched water from the nearby stream, cooked the pig feed, and fed the chickens around their coop calling out "coo coo, coo coo ..." for them to come and eat. The chickens ran to get their feed, clucking noisily in the dark.

It was very cold during the night in the highlands, and my host only gave me a very thin blanket to cover myself. I could not sleep very well, with the cold and all the pre-dawn noise made by the Hmong women. I got out my torch and looked at my watch. It was only four o'clock in the morning. I did not know if I should remain in bed or get up to see what I could help them with, but I did not hear any men's voice as they appeared to all still be in bed. It seemed only the women were up and busy at this ungodly hour, as if these chores were their lot only. Someone was soon chopping grass for the horse and then took it to the horse stable next to the house. The horse sniffed and blew its nose as it ate. Soon, it was the pigs' turn, fighting each other for position along the trough in which warm feed from the giant wok in the bigger family fireplace was poured into. The pigs were growling and hissing in the fog that surrounded the village on the slope of the hill, high up on top of Doi Chiangdao.

In the stillness of the early morning, waiting for the sun to rise in the far eastern horizon, the village was wrapped in thick fog. It was cold, but the Hmong women in this house and all the other houses had already been on their feet for more than an hour working in and out of the house. Soon, they would have to get everything ready, the tools, the backpack baskets and the horses, so they could go early to work in the fields. These toiling and emaciated Hmong women who gave life to their children, were also the ones to renew life daily in their families and the village with this early morning labor. They went about it each day in silence, without protest and without complaints. The men only got up when breakfast was ready, the water to wash their hands and faces was warm in the family hearth, and the first ray of the sun shined on the green leaves on the tree tops at the crest of the hills. Another day had broken, and the repetitive back-breaking farm activities would have to be resumed after breakfast.

Chapter 5

I had now been at the boarding house for nearly two weeks. I was beginning to feel bored and lonely. The place was occupied mostly by passing "Farang" (Western) tourists who were too busy even to make casual conversation so I never got to talk to anyone there, not even the owners. I managed to make conversations with the young cleaning lady who was very nice but too busy with her chores. By the second week, I started to roam the streets of Chiangmai and to enjoy its busy night life. I never got to know where all the bars were, except the ones in the big hotels, but I loved looking at the street stalls and eateries that sprang up at the Evening Bazaar along Surivongs Road, near the boarding house where I was staying. During the day, the area appeared very quiet, but became full of jostling tourists and stall keepers at nightfall.

During this time, I had managed to write once to my mother in America to give her news about what I had been doing and to tell her that I still had not been to Ban Vinai refugee camp to visit Pafua and our many relatives there. I also sent a postcard to Damdouan, but did not have the space to write down my mailing address for her. In the ensuing months, I sent her a few more postcards. I also made other friends and became too absorbed in my new life. I did not try hard enough to keep writing to her, especially after I had gone to the refugee camp and met Pafua. I gradually lost contact with Damdouan, and our relationship seemed to disappear quietly like the evening sun going down behind some red clouds over the far western horizon. Maybe, we were not given the mandate from Heaven to share life with each other, as the Hmong would say in such cases.

One evening I was passing a small hotel. In the midst of all the noise of cars in the street and passers-by walking briskly past each other on the footpath, I heard this familiar voice calling out in Thai, *"Khun, Khun cha pai nai?"* (Mister, where are you going?)

I turned and realized that it was Samanh, the man who forced the prostitute on me more than two weeks ago. He was sitting on his tricycle, parked outside the hotel a few blocks from the one where I first met him. I went over and started chatting with him in his language. He later drove me around in the tricycle looking at the street vendors along the roads while we continued to talk. He asked me where I was staying since he had not seen me at the first hotel anymore. I told him about the boarding house, and about what I was doing in Thailand. He said the boarding house was too expensive and was not a place for me as I was not just a passing Farang tourist. He then took me to his house in the middle of Chiangmai city, near Pratu Changpheuak, to have a cup of tea and to meet his wife. He did not mention any children, but I came to learn months later that he also had another wife with two children in a different part of town.

When we arrived at his house around nine o'clock that night, I noticed that it was a simple timber structure in the Thai style built on stilts with rusty corrugated steel roof. It was on a Soi or side street to one of the main roads running into the eastern canal that surrounded the old royal city of Chiangmai, not far from the Pratu Changpheuak market. Only his young wife and an elderly woman were home, chatting with each other in the lounge room. There was no television, but the room was brightly lit with only a few pieces of plain timber furniture and a multi-colored straw mat on the floor. Samanh introduced them to me, and said that the older woman who looked like being in her fifties cooked and cleaned for them. I did not know that a tricycle driver would be able to afford a cook, but I later learned that she was staying there because she had nowhere to go. Her husband died recently and they did not have any children. Samanh's wife was a plump woman in her late twenties with big dark eyes and a tanned complexion. She greeted visitors with a smile and a generous face as if to say that everything she had was for the taking. After we had finished our tea, Samanh said that if I was not happy at the boarding house I would be welcome to move and stay with them. His house had a spare room and was handy to the TDC. I could help them out with the rent or I could just stay there free. I said I would consider his offer and left to go back to the boarding house.

I was wondering why this man was so generous. Maybe he just
wanted to part me from my money, as people often believed to happen
in Thailand. But I was wrong. I ended up moving into Samanh's house a
few days later and we became great friends. I agreed to pay them rent of
1,000 Baht a month. I informed the TDC director of my move, and he
asked where I was going. When I told him, he looked concerned and
said that I had to be careful about people I associated with, especially
"samlo" drivers. I did not know if he was really concerned or just
condescending towards people he considered of lower social status than
himself. I did not mind that I might have to help Samanh out financially
on many occasions, because he also did many things for me without
thinking about the cost to him. His wife was home most of the time and
was also one of the kindest persons I had met. I liked them both as they
were good company, always chatting with me. She sometimes went out
in the evening on her own, but would tell me that she was visiting
friends in other parts of the city and asked me to help look after the
house. She loved talking and seemed to have many friends, especially
girls who were younger than herself.

On my third day at Samanh's house, three young women visited his
wife. After some conversation, they asked if we could go to the famous
Chiangmai Flower Garden and take some photos. I had brought a
camera with me for my work, and they wanted to try it out. Not wanting
to be seen as unfriendly, I agreed. We set off in a "songtaeo" taxi we
caught on our way to the main street. About halfway there, we were
joined by another young woman named Thiraphorn or Phorn, for short.
She was about my height and had a very slender body. We got on very
well, and it was not long before she came to sit next to me in the taxi
and started to tell me about herself as if we had known each other for
some time. She said that she was a student at Chiangmai University. I
asked her in what faculty and she said "male science." I asked what that
was, and she quickly changed to "social science," making us laugh. I
liked her for her tiny size, her sense of humor and openness — like a
real free spirit.

A week after I took up residence at Samanh's house, he asked if I
would like to go on a trip with him to the country. He was going to visit

his uncle who had fallen off a tree while picking jackfruits and injured himself badly. He was in the hospital for two months, but returned home a few weeks ago. Samanh wanted to go and see how he was doing. I was curious to see the northern Thai country life, so I agreed to go with him, even though this meant I would have to pay for most of the expenses like bus fares and food along the way. We set out very early one morning and went to the Manorod Market near the Maeping River from where we joined a small bus that would take us to San Kampaeng. Samanh's uncle lived not far from this small district town about an hour's drive southeast of Chiangmai city.

It was the middle of the rice harvest season. The fields along the road were yellow with ripening rice stalks extending to the far horizon, and the dust from the dirt road made the irrigation canal along it look red and muddy. Here and there, groups of Thai farmers were cutting the rice plants by hand with sickles, bending down as they cut and getting up to lay the rice stalks into a pile on the rice stumps they had just made. We had to walk part of the way to the village of Samanh's uncle. On the way, we stopped to chat with some young Thai women who were harvesting rice, their heads covered with broad-rimmed hats made from palm leaves. They were all very sun-tanned from working everyday in the open under the hot sun. I took some photos of them, and Samanh told them that I was from America. He sounded very proud to be in the company of such an apparently privileged person, asking the younger girls if they liked me. I was rather embarrassed and did not know what to say. They started asking me about my life in a foreign country, and one of them said that I was beyond their reach because they were just peasant girls who were plain and blackened from their hard farming life. I protested that I liked everyone of them, and they laughed.

We continued on to the village which had about 50 houses of all sizes, mostly built from timber and covered in thatched grass or iron sheets scattered willy-nilly all over the place in between cloves of green bamboos, jackfruit trees and coconut palms. Apart from the odd barking of dogs, the village was quiet, most residents having probably gone to work in the fields or to the market in the next town. We went into a hut with walls and roof protected by layers of broad dry leaves. There were holes on some of the walls where the leaves had fallen off. I was surprised that people were living in it, because it was rather small, no more than 20 square meters in floor space. Samanh said that this was where his uncle's family lived. I could see a thin, emaciated man lying on a bamboo make-shift bed in one corner of the hut, and an elderly woman sitting next to the bed. A second smaller bed was in the other corner, with some folded blankets and clothes on it. There was little else in the hut. They must be cooking outside in the open because there was no fireplace or the semblance of a kitchen inside. I had never seen people living in such dire conditions before in other places.

The man looked up at us when we entered the room, and greeted Samanh and me with a weak smile. Samanh introduced me as his friend, and informed me that these two people were his uncle and aunt. I was shocked to see them living like this, as I had thought that they would have a more decent house. We started chatting about the elderly man's health. He said that although he had improved, he still had pain in his back and had to lie down most of the time. Eventually, the conversation turned to money and it appeared that he owed a lot of money to the hospital in Chiangmai where they took him after his fall from the tree — something like 20,000 Baht for the two months he stayed there. The family did not have any land to farm for a living. The father used to do odd jobs for the village people in return for food or money, but now he could not work anymore and had not been able to earn anything to support his family. I did not know if they hoped I would help them out, but I did not offer anything except to express my sympathy. I hardly knew them, and that was also a lot of money for me. If I lent some to them, how would they repay it?

We had bought some meat and vegetables from town, and stayed for lunch which Samanh's aunt cooked over an earthen stove standing on bamboo planks a few feet above ground outside the hut, with a big terra cotta jar serving as water container next to the stove. She was helped by a young girl who was about 17 years old and who was introduced to me as Duangta, the old couple's youngest daughter. After lunch, Samanh said that we had to go back home before the last bus left for the afternoon. As we made our way out of the hut, Duangta grabbed a little bundle of clothes wrapped in a scarf from the small bed and followed us. I did not know she was coming to Chiangmai with us, so I asked Samanh who said that he had come to get her to go and work with one of his friends in town. He gave me a wink as he was telling me this, but I did not question him further. She was rather short, but with a slim body and tanned skin hidden under a pair of faded jeans and a dotted light green shirt. She appeared to be happy getting away from her parents and going to work in the city.

On the bus, Duangta sat away from Samanh and me at the back. We were in one of the rows of seats in the middle, and there were many other passengers. Without being asked, Samanh started to tell me that Duangta was going to Chiangmai to work as an indentured girl to pay back the money that Samanh had obtained from his friend for her old father's hospital fees. I asked him how many years it would take for her to work to pay her way out of the indenture, and he said, "Maybe four to five years."

"That long for 20,000 Baht? Are you sure that's what it takes?" I asked.

"Well, what can she do? She needs to help her parents out. They are old and have no job or farm to work on. Her father owes money and cannot work because of his poor health. They only have her. She has to show her gratitude to them for bringing her up."

"She is so young. She probably has no work skills and very little education. What work can she do that will earn her enough money?" I asked.

"She hasn't got much choice. In Thailand if you are not born with a silver spoon in your mouth, then you will stay poor. You are not likely to find work that will pay much. Just laboring if you are lucky, but this is usually not for young girls. There is not much work for them in this country, except as servants to rich families. Most of the time, you have to have connections. Many university graduates work as sales assistants in big department stores, and not in offices. Why? Because they have no social or business connections."

"I see. So what work is Ta going to do at your friend's place?"

He hesitated for a while as if he did not know whether to tell me or not. In the end, he said, "What do you think? She will entertain male customers, of course."

"You mean, as a prostitute?"

"Yes, there's no other solution. It's not so bad for girls from the country. Some women get into the business because of money problems with their families, others because they just cannot find any other jobs," he said as if it did not matter at all.

"That's terrible. I think it's a real tragedy for a young girl like Ta. She's probably still a virgin with no experience with men."

"Yes, and that's what the prostitute houses want so the first man will have to pay a lot of money to the house owner. You want to be Ta's first man?" he joked.

"Don't be obscene. I am not a virgin buster or a child molester," I said, feeling helpless about her predicament.

When we arrived in Chiangmai, Samanh took Duangta to the brothel down the road from where we lived, and I did not see her again until a few days later when she came to visit us. It made me feel bad that I could not do anything to help her out of her situation. In the months to come, I learned that the young girls who often visited Samanh's wife were from the so-called house of ill-repute nearby where Ta was now working. At first, I did not want to have anything to do with them, but I later developed much respect for these young women. They seemed to face life's many odds with real courage. Samanh's wife sometimes told me about their personal lives and the plight of their families in the villages which forced them into this line of work. They loved to ask me about life in America and many other subjects, but I tried not to get too close or friendly with them when they were visiting. It was not that I looked down on them. I just did not want them to think I wanted to take advantage of their easy availability, or wanted us to be more than friends.

Chapter 6

A few days following the trip to San Kampaeng, Samanh agreed to accompany me as my guide to Ban Vinai refugee camp, in Loei Province in central northeastern Thailand, to pay my overdue visit to Pafua and other relatives. It had been nearly a month since I arrived in the country. Samanh went to the police to get his identity papers, and did not have much problem with a bit of money under the table. We got on the Chiangmai-Khon Kaen bus. I did not know the way and Samanh was supposed to know. But it turned out that he had never been to this part of Thailand either, so it was like the blind leading the blind. But one good thing about him was that he could ask direction in the local northern Thai dialect and we could always change bus for our next destination. After leaving the Chiangmai bus station, we turned south to follow the same route taken by buses going to Bangkok. Small towns and villages along the route often gave way to open rice paddy fields which adorned the foot of rolling hills that were covered in teak trees and rich tropical vegetation.

Once the bus reached Phitsanulocke, it left the southern highway that lead to Bangkok and turned east to start its journey to northeast Thailand, gradually making its zigzag climb up some of the highest mountains in the country. At that time, much of this area consisted of impenetrable dense forest reserves, the domain of wild elephants and rhinoceros as well as anti-government communist rebels and bandits. Stories were circulating about buses passing through and picking up passengers who turned out to be robbers pointing guns at other passengers and taking all their valuable possessions before forcing the driver to stop and let them out. Houses and rest areas along this part of the route were far and few between until you reached the next provincial town three hours away at Phetchaboon. But on the whole, it was not such a bad trip to make as many other cars also used the route.

After Phetchaboon, the next stop was Lomsak, then Chumpae where the bus would let passengers out for a stretch and lunch. This was also where we had to change to a different bus to go north to Loei where Ban Vinai refugee camp was located. At one point, Samanh asked me where I kept all the money I was taking to relatives in the refugee camp and which was entrusted to me by Hmong families living in America. I told him that it was kept in a bundle in my travelling bag tucked away at the back of the bus. He became angry and scolded me for being so careless. It was carefully locked, but he went to retrieve the bag and kept it between his legs the rest of the journey. It took us nearly two days and four bus changes, going through five provinces before we arrived at Loei, our final destination.

By that time, we looked like dishevelled versions of our former selves — our clothes all creased and dirty. We were covered in dust from head to foot, our hair stood on end from the wind and changed from black to red, and only the white of our eyes shone through mud-crusted eyebrows. That was part of the fun travelling with the ordinary people of Thailand — the smell and dust in the poorer parts of the country. The views were superb and the people nice and friendly, but some of the roads were really dry and dusty, especially in the northeast of the country where drought was prevalent. The old buses used on these roads were often operated by their owners and some were just as old as the owners themselves. The people who used these buses were mostly itinerant workers, traders and villagers who wanted to go to the nearby town to sell or buy some local products. When the bus came to a stop at a town market, food peddlers would rush along the bus windows to show their goods, asking loudly whether anyone wanted to buy something from the tray they carried on their heads or hands, ranging from iced drinks and fruit slices to sticky rice and grilled chicken. Some even came along the aisle of the bus to try and sell directly to the travellers. Because of fear of falling sick from unclean food, I rarely bought anything, but it was nice to hear all the commotion and to look.

A few kilometers before we got to the Ban Vinai refugee camp, five or six Hmong refugees got on the bus and one of the men came to sit next to me. It turned out that he was the husband of one of my distant cousins, and it was a great surprise for both of us to meet after more

than ten years. Vang-yu was his name. He used to be a captain in the
CIA secret army in Laos. Unlike many other Hmong who were
conscripted into this army of about 5,000 men strong, Vang-yu had
joined voluntarily and was lucky to have got out alive when it was
estimated that 15,000 of them had died fighting against the North
Vietnamese and Pathet Lao communist soldiers between 1961 and 1972.
And now, he was living in Ban Vinai refugee camp with his wife and four
children. He was a strong, stout man, with short crew-cut hair and had
on a wide-brimmed hat made from dry palm leaves to protect himself
from the sun at the farm where they had just returned from. I told him
that I was going to the refugee camp. He said he was returning from
working for some local Thai farmers to earn money to supplement the
small ration they were getting from the United Nations High
Commission for Refugees. When we got off the bus at the entrance to
the camp, he insisted that Samanh and I stay at his house.

Although I had many relatives and friends in the camp, I realized
once I arrived there that I really did not know where they lived. I did
not know the camp was so big, covering many acres. It housed more
than 40,000 refugees, sprawling across rolling hills along three small
creeks. There was a hospital and a market serving the camp population,
but only one school for thousands of children, most of whom could not
be enrolled and spent their days just playing or doing nothing. The camp
was divided into six sections, with the main buildings comprising long
houses raised on timber floors and covered with corrugated iron roofing.
Each building was divided into six rooms, with each room allocated to a
family without regard to how many people were in it. At the back and
aligned to each room in the main building were the kitchens which
consisted of timber huts built by the refugees themselves — some big
and some small, depending on the resources and taste of each family.

Beyond the camp to the west were mountains covered in thick
forests broken by clearings which were used by the local Thai villagers
as dry rice or corn fields. Above the camp stood a high peak of greyish
rocky outcrops overlooking the camp buildings and their inhabitants
like a divine protective sight. The camp area had been cleared of most
of the vegetation, save some clumps of tall trees here and there that

were kept for shade. It was surrounded by grassy hills that stretched in a criss-crossing fashion all the way to the Mekong River about five kilometers away to the east. The dirt road that linked Pakchom to Loei went past the camp, sending clouds of thick red dust into the houses near its boundary fence every time a car or bus drove by.

Vang-yu said, "Stay with me for a few days, then you can go to your relatives once we find out where they live."

"Thank you. I suppose I have no other way," I said to show him my relief and appreciation. "I would not know where to go and ask, especially with all this luggage."

We started walking from the bus stop at the entrance to the camp, and passed through a check point manned by Thai soldiers who did not really check anyone. There were also many Thai women from the local villages who were selling vegetables, firewood and other goods along the road into the camp. I had never seen so many Hmong people in my life. The dirt road was teeming with women, men and children going or coming from somewhere. After about one kilometer and with bags on our backs and in our hands, we finally arrived at Vang-yu's house in Section Number 4 of the camp. I was shown where to have a bath, using water from an old steel barrel near a well on the bank of a small creek not far from the house. I felt so much lighter after divesting myself of all the dust and dirt from nearly two days of bus travelling, and enjoying for the first time the sweet smell of bathing soap.

I did not want to show how eager I was to visit Pafua, so I waited until the next day. Vang-yu knew which building her family was living in, as he often visited a cousin there. He went with me to show the way. My heart was beating in anticipation of meeting the young refugee girl I had come so far to see and of whom my mother had such high regard. I really did not know what would be the right things, the first words I should say to her after all the letters we had written to each other. To my great disappointment and also relief, we discovered that she and her mother were not home but had gone to Loei, the provincial town that we passed through the day before about 60 kilometers away. I left them a message and spent the rest of the day visiting other acquaintances in different parts of the camp, and returned to Vang-yu's house in the evening. I was hoping that Pafua would come and look for me, having learned of my arrival and where I was staying from her neighbor. But no, she did not make an appearance and I was left to wonder what she really felt about me.

Early the next day, I again went to Pafua's house with Samanh. The first thing I saw of her was her back turning towards the door. She was preparing rice for cooking in a pot and was busy washing it. Her mother invited us in and asked us to sit down. By this time Pafua had turned to face us, and got up from her crouching position. We had never met before and as I had expected, we did not quite know how to react to each other. I had only seen her photo, but now I was facing her in person and I really liked her. She was shorter than me, had rather angular facial features and long black hair left hanging loose around her shoulders and back, like in her photograph. Her body was somewhat on the full side like a full-grown young woman but seemed to suit her perfectly. Her skin, like that of her mother, was very fair. She had on a long maroon Lao skirt like a sarong that went down to her ankles, and a white blouse with very short sleeves — it being very hot in the camp with temperatures in the mid-thirty degrees centigrade even at that time in October.

Pafua did not smile, but gave the usual polite Hmong greeting to visiting strangers by saying, *"Neb tuaj xyuas peb los."* (You have come to visit us.)

She then asked where I had come from. She had a nice soft voice and very polite manners. I told her I was Mua from the United States and that we had been writing to each other.

"When did you arrive in Thailand?" she asked, her face suddenly brightening up and beaming with her first smile. She appeared to be as excited as I was about our meeting each other at last. It was as if she had been waiting for my arrival, although I did not tell her exactly which day I would get to the refugee camp as I did not have the means to inform her quickly. I replied that I arrived two days before, and started to apologize about how long I had been in Thailand but was not able to come earlier. Her mother had aged a lot in the 18 years or so since I last saw her with Pafua's father in Muang Khun. She looked like a woman who was used to a better life but had obviously been through difficult times in recent years — being in a polygamous marriage with the new husband and having to fend for herself and her children most of the time had certainly not been easy.

"You got here two days ago. How was your trip, Mua?" she asked me in a kindly, mother-like voice. She probably knew my name from her daughter after we started writing to each other.

"The trip was good, thank you, aunty. We came to see you yesterday, but you were not home," I said.

"Pafua needed some material and we went to Loei to buy it for her. We did not know you had come. No one told us."

"But I did ask one of the neighbors to tell you," I replied and was rather discouraged to hear what she said.

"They were probably too busy and forgot."

I felt much better. All my misconception about Pafua's not looking me up yesterday disappeared. After all, we had not met before and it might not be proper for her to come searching for me. We then chatted about many little subjects, about my mother and how she was coping in America after going there five months earlier. About an hour later, the lunch that Pafua was preparing was near ready, and I did not know whether to stay on and let them invite me to eat, or whether I and Samanh should leave and come back later. In the end, I decided to leave. I had the feeling that Pafua was very shy with me at this first meeting, following the initial greetings. She hardly said anything much, after our initial introduction. It was mainly her mother who made conversation with me. They were not very persistent with their invitation for us to join them for lunch, and I did not want to embarrass them in case they thought their refugee food was not good enough for me. After promising to return in the late afternoon, we went to the local market, had some noodle there, and took a walk around in the market looking at Hmong needlecrafts. I then went to visit some relatives on the other side of the market.

About four o'clock in the afternoon, I returned to see Pafua but she was not home. Her mother said that she had just gone to get firewood with some friends up the top of the hill overlooking the camp. I did not

know how to get there or how long she would be gone, so I said to her
mother that I would come back in the evening or the next day. By this
time, many people had heard that a Hmong person from America was in
the camp for the very first time, and they wanted to see me to ask
questions about how they could apply to go and live in the US. Because
of the Hmong's previous involvement with the CIA-supported anti-
communist army in Laos, the American government was accepting many
of them to start a new life in America. But rumors were ripe that
American men forced married Hmong women to sleep with them or
even their dogs, that dead bodies were cut up during autopsies and used
as canned pet food, and that many sick refugees were medically
experimented on and died. People in the camp were very interested to
know the real situation from a Hmong who had lived in that country in
person for many years and whose family recently joined him. I was
invited to one of my cousin's house and got to talking to a group of these
refugees, and did not get the time to visit Pafua again as I said earlier to
her mother.

Chapter 7

The next morning when I got to her house, Pafua was there by herself. I was happy to see her without her mother, whose presence seemed to intimidate us somewhat the previous day. I apologized for not coming the previous evening. She was sitting on the porch of the main building and was busy doing some kind of Hmong embroidery.

"It does not matter. You don't need to apologize. You have other things to do," she observed.

This time she seemed to be so nice, understanding and less inhibited. Dressed in a yellow blouse and a pair of purple slacks, she looked like a fresh sunflower that stood out among the dwarf dahlias around her in these squalid surroundings. She got up to go to the kitchen to get me some drink, but I said that she did not need to as I already had some at Vang-yu's house. She insisted that what I just had was not hers and now that I was in her house she should offer me her own drink, even if it was only plain water. The refugee camp was always a busy and noisy place with people coming and going, or chatting in groups outside their kitchens and in front of their buildings. It was getting hot, but where we were it was quiet like an island of peace and calm. It made me want to prolong my stay with her, and I was trying to think about what to say to her to make our conversation last as long as possible so that I did not have to go away for a few hours.

After she returned with a glass of water for me, I took it from her and said, "You're very nice, like my mother told me. I am sorry that we don't have enough time to be with each other."

"Well, we don't need a lot of time. You'll probably be very bored just being with me all the time. So many other people also want to see and talk to you about going to America."

"Yes, but I came to the camp especially for you," I replied, feeling rather guilty.

I wanted to get to the point, since we had already been writing to each other for some time. I did not have much time to remain in the camp before I had to go back to Chiangmai to start my work with the Tribal Development Center. I only had 12 months in Thailand and nearly four weeks had already gone by.

"We haven't met for long. But you know, I really like you," I added.

"Really? You are not just being polite?"

"No, I really do," I replied.

"Well, maybe you do, otherwise you would not have sent me money and come such a long way to see me," she acknowledged, not full of arrogance and pride but with modesty in her voice.

I could not talk about love. I was not sure how we felt about each other, as it was only our second meeting. Somehow, I had to get to know her better, so I asked her about her life in the camp, what she did most days and so on. She told me that there was nothing much to do since she came back from learning dress-making in Oudontani. Sometimes, she would go to Loei, the nearest city, to spend the day there watching a movie and shop, but preferred to spend most of her time attending to the cooking and household chores of the family, being the eldest daughter. Sometimes, she liked listening to Thai music or read Thai women's magazines she bought on her trips to Loei

At that point, I realized that I had not sent her any money for some time, so I got 2,000 Baht out from my wallet and gave the money to her. She did not accept it, but said that I had many other relatives to give it to and she was all right, she did not need any money. I knew that was not true. I knew from my past correspondence and her previous requests that her financial situation was far from good, as she had no income — like so many other refugees in the camp. I ended up giving the money to her mother who did not seem to put up so much resistance. I reasoned that perhaps she thought it improper to accept money from me face-to-face, and yet what I could not understand was that she did not refuse what I sent her through the post. I later learned that she only refused out of politeness, but I did not realize it then.

Over the next few days, I continued to visit Pafua. She became less shy and we seemed to be able to make better conversations. I also agreed to join in the family meals on a few occasions. Her mother usually left us alone to talk in the kitchen which seemed to serve also as the family's living room while the only room allocated to them in the main building was used mostly as the bedroom. I now had been in the camp for more than a week and only had a few days left. One day, I asked if she would like to go to a movie in Loei, maybe with her sister and younger brother or some other friends. She did not accept immediately, but said she would think about it. I said to her that I would get permission from the Thai camp commander for her and her friends so we could go outside for a day together. I was feeling closer to her and wanted to find different ways to enjoy her company as well as to give her time to get away from the oppressive crowding in the camp.

Two days later, we went to Loei. On the rattling old bus, she sat next to her younger sister, opposite me. I did not mind. She was probably reluctant to sit next to me because she did not want people to spread gossip about us. Samanh also came, and when we got to Loei, he went to get the tickets for the movie. As usual, we were all covered in dust from the dirt on the road and the two hour journey, but we just brushed it off the best we could. I was feeling itchy and uncomfortable, because it was very hot besides being very dusty. But people around me seemed to be oblivious to all the smell, the heat and the rubbish along the roads in Loei, so I tried my best to act as if there was nothing unusual. The streets were full of life. Like every town in Thailand, people were talking loudly to each other, riding motorcycles with splattering engine noise, or walking along the shopping area almost bumping into each other. As usual, the sound of car horns and car engines dominated all other noises, but you soon got used to it all.

The movie house was old and dusty like everything else in the town, but at least it had cement-rendered walls and a tile roof. The seats were old, but not too smelly and tatty like those on the bus. There were six of us and we sat at the back of the room, spread out in one row. This time Samanh helped to make sure that I got a seat next to Pafua at the end of the row. The movie was a Hong Kong Chinese love story with voice-over in the Thai language. They were all very absorbed in the movie, but I was busy thinking how I could improve my relationship with Pafua. I have been in the refugee camp for nearly two weeks, and not much progress seemed to have been made. I do not mean that she should have let me touch her or jump into bed with her. No, my worry was that she appeared to be rather distant sometimes when we were together. The only difference after our first meeting was that she now talked more openly with me, but showed no other signs of affection or love.

In the dark of the movie house, I slowly slipped my right hand to touch her left one on her lap. To my great surprise, she did not withdraw her hand from mine, but kept still as if nothing happened. After a few seconds which seemed like an eternity, I gathered up enough courage to squeeze her hand and then to entwine her fingers in mine. Again to my joy, she squeezed back, never flinching or looking at me. Her eyes were kept on the big screen, as if trying to concentrate on the story being unfolded there. My mind was, however, fully on the story being unravelled on her lap. I was so happy that she was at last showing some positive reaction.

After we returned from Loei, our relationship did show a lot of the right signs like she would ask me questions about myself and the work that was waiting for me in Chiangmai. She seemed to show more interest in me, the way I had shown towards her. Sometimes when we were alone in her family's kitchen, she would let me touch her small hands or her soft face. The day finally came when I had to reluctantly return to Chiangmai to get on with the other work I had come to Thailand for. I told Pafua that we still had a few months in Thailand to see more of each other, and if things worked out we would get married and I would apply for her and her family to go to live with me in America. Or maybe, she could come and stay with me in Chiangmai if we got married before I finished my work there.

She merely replied, "Good, we will see."

I was again surprised by this very cool response. I could not understand this changing attitude from one day or situation to another, especially after all the positive signs of the last few days we had spent together. However, I put it all to her feminine modesty and the Hmong culture which requires "good girls" to act with reluctance and cool-headedness towards men.

She and her mother along with many other relatives came to the bus stop to see me and Samanh off. She did not seem too concerned seeing me go up north and knowing that we would not see each other again for another two or three months. She just stood on the side of the road, looking at me as the bus pulled out and not even waving goodbye or smiling or looking sad. I was completely confused, but maybe I had become too westernized in my thinking. Maybe I had read too many Western books, seen too many Hollywood movies about love and been away from the Hmong people for too long? Perhaps, my extension work in Chiangmai among the traditional Hmong villagers there might help me to understand the Hmong culture better? And yet, I could not help thinking that she was not a traditional village girl, she was the daughter of urbanized middle-class Hmong parents who sent her to school in the city in Laos and later in Thailand. She could not be so traditional and reacted to my departure in this way. Maybe she did not really click with me or had found someone better? I was asking myself these questions as the bus left for Loei where we had to change to a new bus for Chumpae and then Chiangmai. The engine of the bus that was probably rarely serviced, was struggling noisily under the bonnet as the old transporter made its way up a steep stretch of the dirt road. But I did not hear its struggle for breath. I was too absorbed in my thoughts remembering Pafua and her family.

Chapter 8

The first thing I found when we got back to Samanh's home from our visit to Pafua at Ban Vinai was Phorn sitting in the lounge room chatting with Samanh's wife and two other girls who were also visiting. After the initial words of greetings, I did not pay much attention to them, as I was tired from the long bus journey. But I was wrong. As soon as Samanh put my bag in my room and left, Phorn breezed in and asked if I wanted to go to the movies with her. I never thought of seeing her again after the visit to the Flower Garden. I had not gone further with her than taking photos of her and her three friends, and chatting in the taxi. Maybe Samanh's wife had told her a lot more about me than I knew, I was saying to myself. Now she was showing signs that we were more than just casual acquaintances.

She had a very short and body-hugging green dress on, making every feature of her small body stand out, including a rather small chest. She did not have a lot of make-up on like the first time I saw her.

She came over and sat on the bed.

"I have been waiting for you so many days. I thought you would never come back," she said.

"Oh, I have to return to work in Chiangmai."

"Since we went to the Flower Garden, I have been waiting to see when we will meet again," she went on.

I had to be polite with her, I thought to myself.

"It's nice to know you want to meet me again," I said.

"Don't pretend we are strangers. I told you a lot about myself during our first meeting, and now I want to know you. I can only do that if you take me out so we have time to talk and enjoy ourselves," she continued.

"Maybe we can go another time. I am very tired today," I explained as gently as I could.

"Why can't we go just for a short little while?"

I was beginning to get tired of her persistence when I already gave her the reason, but I did not want to spoil things for her that day when she looked so happy. She soon glided over with her slick body and grabbed me by the arm. She was stomping one of her small feet on the timber floor like a spoilt child and shaking her body in the process.

"Please, please come with me. I was so looking forward to it and have planned it for the last few days since I knew you were coming back," she said.

I suddenly found this woman transformed into a young girl, so full of charm, so child-like, and all my resistance melted away.

"Alright, just today. But I have to wash and get changed first."

"Oh, you are so nice," she said, looking triumphant.

Her face suddenly lit up with joy. She squeezed my hand in appreciation, then went to join her friends in the lounge room again.

We rode in a taxi through some noisy streets to go to the cinema at the southern side of the wide canal around the old royal compound of Chiangmai city. After we arrived, Phorn chose a Thai love story in which the heroine was a country girl who fell in love with the town's rich boy, was used and left with a baby to take care of while he went abroad to study. In her roaming in and out of her house and the Thai countryside waiting for her prince charming, the heroine's tears could have filled a bucket — and Phorn's tears could have also filled half of one. I must admit I also shed some tears against my own will. We left the movie house, all red-eyed and went on for a late night supper at some big expensive hotel nearby where we talked until the small hours about life, about ourselves some more and about me, as Phorn had said. I was surprised that I had so much fun with this rather scatter-brained little woman. Time went by quickly and I almost wished that we did not have to go home so soon.

A few days later, I was finally given long-term extension work to do at a Hmong village located on the slope of Doi Sanpa, one of the highest mountains in northern Thailand on top of which the Royal Thai Army and the American Central Intelligence Agency were said to have installed a radar station to track American military aircraft movements from Thailand during the Vietnam War. The villagers were White Hmong and mostly opium growers like so many other hill tribe people at the time. The United Nations Drug Replacement Program had started a project to introduce alternative cash crops to the opium farmers there so that they could give up growing the illicit drug. I got on well with the villagers and the Thai staff working on the project. I spent the next few months working with them to evaluate the benefits of cash crops being propagated by the project to the village, and to teach Hmong farmers about their cultivation with my Thai counterpart.

The village was called Maewang and had 40 families with close to 200 people living in three settlements about one or two kilometers from each other. Less than ten of the families were planting rice for their own consumption. The rest of the villagers relied on growing opium to sell or exchange for food and other necessities. Two of the households had a large number of cattle, but others only kept pigs and chickens. Nearly all the households were involved in the United Nations opium replacement project. The village headman, Zong Cheng, was related by clan name to my mother and treated me like a son. The UN project had built a school in the village, but the 30 or so boys and girls attending the school were only starting their first three years of primary studies. The headman was pleased that a young Hmong like me had gone past primary school and was able to obtain university degrees in America. He was impressed and willing to ask the village people to help me with my extension work among them.

My Thai counterpart and I travelled to the project site by car half way up Doi Sanpa where the road ended, and then went on foot the rest of the journey. There was no road to the village yet in those days. We stayed at the UN compound during the week, then slipped back to town for the weekend if we needed to. During this time, I also wrote a few letters to Pafua in the refugee camp, always saying how much I missed her and would be coming to visit her again in a month or so. I only received one reply from her, a very short one about one page long telling me how she was doing and how her family was coping and thanking me for the money I sent her after I returned from my visit. I really did miss her, especially on those weekends back in town when I spent most of my free time by myself without Phorn.

Maybe, it was also guilt, as I was being drawn more and more to the night life in Chiangmai and to Phorn. After the movies, there would be the late night dances — at first only fast and furious numbers but gradually ending with slow, dreamy ones. She was a really fun person with a keen sense of the real world. When we were together, we seemed to forget all our worries and troubles, shutting out all the things we wished to forget. What really bothered me was that during those hours I was with Phorn on the hotel dance floor or the smoky drinking area, I never thought of Pafua. Only afterwards or the next day. We were careful not to get drunk, and we never went anywhere for anything more than just trying to have fun with movies and dancing. She made me feel like I was special to her, a young man she enjoyed keeping company with and whom she could talk to. And I started to see her in a new light, not just a dance companion or a drinking friend but a white camellia in full bloom which seemed so frail you dared not touch in case its white petals would be spoiled, wither and die.

Chapter 9

One evening, Phorn took me to this very expensive hotel called the Lanna, near the foot of Doi Suthep not far from Chiangmai University. It was recently completed in traditional Thai architecture and oozed real high-class luxury. After sitting down at the bar and ordering some soft drink, I asked her how she came to know such a place. She said she was living not far from there in a student dormitory, and walked past the hotel many times on her way to the University.

We continued to talk and compare notes about university life for some time. We also danced a few slow numbers played by the hotel band. When it was close to midnight, Phorn got up and went to the hotel reception. I did not know what she was doing, but saw her get a room key. She seemed very friendly with the receptionists at the desk the way they were chatting as if they knew each other. She was smiling at them and standing there talking for a few minutes, then disappeared into the public toilet on the far side of the hotel lobby.

She came back after a few moments and said, "Are you ready to go?"

"Yes, where are we going?" I asked her.

"Just follow me. I'll show you."

She led me to the hotel lift, and we went up to the third floor. I did not know what she wanted to show me, but she seemed to know which room to go to. I did not ask her anything, I just followed her. I guessed she wanted to do something she had wanted for some time, so I just kept following her. I knew it was not the time to ask questions. I did not want to embarrass her and ruin something she had probably taken a lot of pain and courage to prepare. Once in the room, she put the "please do not disturb" sign on the outside door knob and carefully locked the door. I also would have to pay for this expensive room, probably three times the cost of hotels I normally used. But it did not seem to matter then.

Phorn stretched out her arms and welcomed me in them. We started kissing at first gently then furiously, and she tasted really sweet and good. Her mouth and lips were like drops of tropical morning dew, soft and rolling this way and that as if to savor every little movement before the hot sun made them disappear. Her small body was quivering like a blade of grass being made love to by the gentle afternoon breeze on the slope of some undulating hills in the highlands. She must be as nervous as I was, consumed by the excitement of something we had long anticipated but never quite knowing what it would turn out to be like in reality. Unlike in the movies, we did not leave a trail of clothes on the floor on the way to the queen size hotel bed at one end of the large room we found ourselves in. I carried her there fully clothed, lay her down on the luxurious quilt on the bed, and continued kissing her. She opened her mouth and our lips were making sweet melodies of love and enchantment, exploring and savoring the fragrant taste of each other. I put my right hand on her breasts one after the other, touching them and feeling them, small but soft and full, like the exquisite feel of thin balloons filled with pliable jelly and their little dark knobs looking like the pointed end of a Hmong mouth harp being entwined by skilled fingers to make beautiful musical notes, each sound carrying its own different love message and meaning.

Phorn was silent and yielding. Her hands were roaming my back, my face and my neck, as if wanting to explore treasures of her own. Hers was a different touch, a different sphere of life, a new step to the door of paradise. It was like love being exchanged, being sought and given without expecting anything in return. We were eager and desperate. The music of love has no sound, and only lovers hear it and know its silent language from the firmament of their ecstasy and the delight of their flesh. The world turns, spinning the lovers to dizzy tumultuous heights. For the two of us, that sweet moment was not paid sex and yet it was not like love. It seemed like despair, long pent-up feelings of too much waiting and hoping. We went for it like two hungry beasts tearing at and fighting for the same prey. After a while, she stopped touching me, and then suddenly let out a loud wail as if she was in pain. I stopped dead, but she motioned me to continue, all the while she was wailing like a wounded animal and tears were streaming down her face. Sobs were coming out of her throat like she was strangling and fighting for breath.

I did not know what to do but to plow forward. We were like two raging rivers flowing into a bigger one, bursting its banks and causing a flood beyond anyone's control. At one point, someone was knocking on the door, maybe a hotel guard suspecting domestic violence in the room. But we were too busy to pay attention, and he went away. Her wailing gradually subsided as we were nearing the point of finishing. Afterwards when we had a good rest, I told her that she was wailing so loud she scared me. Phorn just laughed, not saying a word. She never explained why and I let it go at that. I had never been with a woman who reacted so strongly and in such a strange way to this pleasing aspect of the human life. Other women might sigh and moan, but to wail and cry with real tears was something I had not come across before. But to yield in love is like to be born again, releasing the deepest feelings in the center of our soul for the loved one and knowing fully that the delight of the act will outlast its pain.

Phorn decided to take a shower, and I joined her. For the first time, I saw her nude body to the full. It was starting to show some signs of time on her front, but it had a very special beauty of its own. Her breasts were beginning to sag and a few wrinkles had appeared here and there on her stomach but it was still flat with no sign of any fat. What she lacked on the chest, she made up with two beautiful round buttocks which were as appealing as those on younger girls. After the shower, we returned to the room.

While drying ourselves with the hotel's thick towels, I asked her how old she was, and she replied, "Twenty something. What about you?"

"Twenty something, too."

We both fell on the bed, giggling like two children who had just committed some naughty act.

"You seem to know the people working here well," I remarked, curious about the way she was talking to the receptionists in the hotel lobby earlier.

"No, I don't know them. I was nervous like hell, but I wanted to do it, to get a room for us. It was like a dare for myself, you see. It took me a while because they were asking me for my personal details."

"You little devil, I didn't know you were up to these sorts of games," I said catching her in my arms and rolling with her on the bed.

All night long, it seemed I could never have enough of her. She never denied me any place I wanted to touch, her face, her mouth and its small lips, her dark eyes that looked so deep and beautiful, her slender body and skinny legs. I was fondling her and admiring her, and she was happy for me to do it, she was giving up herself to me to enjoy and to admire like a child clutching his first toy. Soon, we were in a tangle and making love again. We did it on the floor, standing up, crouching, in the armchair, on the table, and then on the bed again — it seemed to happen everywhere and to go on and on, so many times as if it was beyond control and we were not ourselves but some mechanical beings trying to outperform each other, but her responses were now more tame and she did not wail like the first time again. It was daylight before we were too dead tired and fell asleep.

I woke up about nine in the morning to find Phorn still in deep sleep with nothing on. I took a closer look at her face, and it looked really peaceful and happy. I covered her with a blanket, and went to take a shower. I noticed that I could hardly walk. I had had five hours of sleep but I still felt like I was walking in my sleep. Was that what too much love and physical exertion did to you?

When I returned from the shower, Phorn was awake but still lying in bed. I said to her teasingly, "Get up, sleepy head. We did not return home last night, and nobody knows where we are. They are going to wonder what has happened to us. Next thing, the police will be looking for us all over town."

She just giggled like a child. I went over to her, and asked, "Did you have a nice time? Are you happy?"

"Yes, very happy, for a long time."

I did not want to spoil her fun by asking why "for a long time." Instead, I touched her on her chin, looked at her in the eyes and said, "You know, it was the most beautiful night of my life last night."

"Yes, for me, too. I never thought it could be so good," she commented.

"Really? Maybe, it's you and the room," I said and moved to her side of the bed to cuddle her in my arms.

"Sometimes you get to know a person really well sleeping together. I think I know you more in one night than all the time we have been together the past few weeks," she said, almost as if musing to herself.

"Yes, that's so true. When you give without holding back, you really know how good you are for each other," I said, turning her face towards me and brushing my hand on her shiny black hair.

For a long time, we continued chatting like that, comfortable and at peace in each other's arms and listening to each other's breathing and the sound of the traffic from outside the hotel room. I was feeling very happy at that moment, as if all my hopes and life dreams had been fulfilled and I had no other cravings to satisfy. I did not think about other people, or about Pafua. I was contented to be with Phorn, to do what we enjoyed doing with each other and not to think about anything else, not to ruin these tender moments of togetherness. About ten o'clock, we got dressed and went downstairs where I paid 600 Baht at the desk for the room. I still felt dead tired — like someone had put me through a boxing ring and smashed me up from head to foot, but I also felt very happy. I asked Phorn if she felt exhausted, but she said that she was feeling great because she had a really good sleep. I was thinking that maybe men and women were not made the same, like some people say after all.

Chapter 10

The following week I went back to Ban Vinai to visit Pafua. After the good time I had with Phorn, I started to feel guilty that I seemed to have forgotten the girl in the refugee camp. I was telling myself that what happened between me and Phorn was not love, but just some feelings of physical need and maybe loneliness on both our parts. After our night at the hotel, I went back to the village and did not get to see Phorn again. I did think a lot about what happened, but I reasoned that was because of the unusual experience rather than because I was missing her company. She was a really sweet and giving little person who appeared so frail in body and yet so strong in spirit. She looked like she needed love and protection, but could also give them equally in return. Maybe Pafua could do even better if only I had more time to spend with her.

When I arrived at Ban Vinai, I went to stay with a cousin named Lychu in Section Number 6 of the camp next to the dirt road to Loei. Pafua seemed happy seeing me again on this second visit, and let me touch her arms and hands freely when no one was around. As I was thinking of her as my future wife rather than some girl I met and had fun with in passing, I never went beyond looking at her and holding her hands briefly now and then when no one could see. I was happy that she seemed more open and our relationship was going in a less subdued way. Unlike during my first visit, she seemed to be more willing and ready to let the sparks of love fly between us.

In between visits to Pafua, I also saw a lot of other families who knew me and who had some interesting stories to tell. I was recording their refugee experiences so that I could write articles about them later as part of my research interests. In the process, I got to know the Thai camp commander from whom I had to seek permission to visit and talk to the refugees. He was a tall man, who used to be in the Thai border army, but very approachable and nice. He showed a lot interest in what I was going to do in Chiangmai. A Thai intelligence police in Chiangmai later told me that they knew all about where I went and what I did in the refugee camp, and I suspected the camp commander had something to do with informing them, but I did not care much about it. After all, I had not done anything illegal.

One day I asked Pafua if she would like to go to the movies or to do some shopping at Loei. She said she would but would like to ask a friend to come with us. I said that would be fine. The next day when we were ready to go, Pafua told me that her friend became unwell and excused herself for not being able to come with us. It was too sudden to obtain written permission from the camp commander's office for a new person to accompany us. I asked Pafua if she still would like to go and she said we had wasted all that time and money to obtain permission for her, and that she would like to go just for the day if it was alright with her mother. Eventually, everything was sorted out with her family who seemed to think that it would not be improper for the two of us to take a day out together, since we were likely to end up getting married anyway. I was rather proud that they had such trust in me. I was 26 years of age at the time, and Pafua was younger than me by eight years. I was seen as educated and responsible, wise and clear-headed with a big measure of respectability and a great future. Anyone who had been to study in a Western country was seen in this light by many envious Hmong, whether the person met their expectations or not. And I always tried to live up to this image trusted on me by other people — something which was not always easy but often with its own small rewards and privileges.

Pafua and I went to Loei on the early bus in the morning and we arrived there about ten — again covered in dust from head to foot. She had a white blouse on, and it was simply ruined by the trip. It now looked like it had been dragged through the street, making her look like someone who had just finished work in the garden rather than someone who had come to the city to shop. I told her that I would buy her new clothes to put on before we decided what to do for the rest of the day. After we got the new clothes from a small clothing store, it dawned on us that we had nowhere for her to get changed. I asked her whether she would mind if we went to a hotel.

"That would be too expensive just to get changed, and it wouldn't look good," she said.

"I know, but what can we do? No one here knows us, and the hotel will just be for you to have a wash and to change into the new clothes. In any case, I am a very square person, I would not do anything to my future wife until after her wedding. I want her to remain pure, untainted. If you want, I won't even go in and wait for you outside," I joked with her, but really believing what I said.

In the end, she relented and we went to one of the cheaper hotels opposite the main market in Loei. We only had a shopping bag containing Pafua's new clothes and the reception clerk was giving us an understanding familiar look as if we were there only to use the hotel bed. Pafua appeared rather embarrassed but I told her not to mind. When we got to the room on the first floor, I opened the door and asked if she wanted me to stay outside. She said maybe it would not be safe for me to do that, and perhaps I should go into the room to keep her company because she might not be safe in the room by herself either — someone might be in the cupboard or climb in through the window to do something to her. We both went in and I washed my face, neck and arms quickly before going over to sit on the chair by the window looking down at the people coming and going at the market opposite. There were many tricycles in front of the market entrance, and one would go while another came in to take its place in the parking line.

I did not know how long I was looking at the traffic below. Pafua was very quiet in the shower and getting changed, and I never tried to look for fear she might get too embarrassed. When I heard her move in the room, I thought that she had finished putting on her new clothes and was ready for us to go out. I turned to look and there, she was standing in the middle of the room, fully dressed in her new cream-colored slacks and plain red shirt. She looked really refreshed, and beautiful with her short frame and really white soft skin. She did not seem to have changed from the shy innocent girl I had known on my first visit, but she now appeared to be a more confident young woman. I was wondering how long it took her to make herself look so good in the bathroom.

I did not know what else to do, but before I could find something to say, she asked, "Would you like to take a proper shower? The water is nice and cool. It feels so good after our long, hot, dusty trip. You want to try?"

I was touched by her care and concern. I had thought up to then that perhaps she did not care very much for me. She had not said anything like that before.

"No, maybe we'd better go and do your shopping. We have to get back on the bus by three o'clock this afternoon," I said.

She went to sit on the bed and pulled down the yellow towel that was still wrapped around her hair.

"We have enough time. Have a shower first," she said in a very sweet and gentle voice.

I gave in. This was something I had not anticipated, but was not probably an invitation to stay on in the hotel and do other things. I was trying to find what best to say or to do under the situation; it seemed that I was always slow when it came to girls I really cared about, and I had lost many good opportunities in the past.

Before I knew it, I had said to her, "Yes, we are always in a hurry. We are forever afraid of what other people think, always controlled by them. Maybe, we should take our time today. We don't have many chances like this."

"Yes, if you like," her answer came back, returning to its usual flat, non-committal tone.

In the shower, I was thinking to myself that for the first time since we met, she was saying something which showed she cared for me. She wanted me to have a shower and to cool down from the hot Thai summer heat. Of course, she had let me hold her hands before, but she had not said anything like she did on this occasion. I was wondering if she had begun to show real feelings of love for me.

After the shower, I found her sitting on the chair by the window, looking down at the market the way I was doing earlier. I walked quietly to where she was sitting with her back towards me. I put out my hands tenderly over her eyes. I did not touch her anywhere else for fear she might get offended — being a Hmong girl and all. She was rather slow to react, almost like the first time I squeezed her hands in the darkened cinema. This made me want to try to kiss her. She seemed to be surprised and did not know what to do. Then she disengaged herself from me, and said that we should be going. She did not show that she was pleased or angry. She just walked towards the door as if to say that it did not matter. In a way, I was relieved that it ended this way and did not lead to other things like it might have been with Phorn. But it also made me confused, after what I was thinking about her in the shower less than five minutes ago. All the same, I felt very tender towards her and it never occurred to me that we would do anything more than touching hands, for if we were going to get married we would have a life time to get to know each other and to enjoy doing things with each other. There was no need to rush and do something which might be seen as premature and wrong in her eyes.

After leaving the hotel and before doing more shopping, I asked if Pafua would like to go for a walk in the local park opposite the District Administration Office. There were a lot of flowers there, and it would be nice to take some photos of ourselves. I had taken photos of Pafua and her family at the refugee camp, but not somewhere with a nice and colorful background. We went to the park in a tricycle, about five minutes from the main market. It was very nice being in the tricycle with Pafua, as we had to squeeze ourselves onto its small seat. I did not know how she would react if I put my arm around her, so I hesitated for few moments before I decided to do it. She did not react in any way at all, just letting my right arm resting on her lower back and my hand on her side. She felt very soft, her new clothes rustling against my skin and smelling nice and new — like the way she felt nice and new to me at that moment. It was as if she had turned a new leaf on that day with me, as if she was a beautiful piece of Hmong embroidery which had just been taken out of a locked trunk and unravelled on a table for all to touch and admire. And I was lucky to be the only person around that table at the time.

She was a little embarrassed when we alighted at the park, but I pretended that nothing was happening and we walked into the center of the park where there was a fountain and a long concrete pond. There were flowers in flower beds scattered throughout the park, mostly red and white in colour. I did not really know their names. We looked at the pond and there was a lot of little colorful fish swimming in the clear water. We did not bring anything with us to feed the fish with, so we only looked at them. Pafua was very interested in the fish, as if she had not seen anything like them before. She kept looking at them and admiring their many colors. It seemed that this was the first time I saw her smiling, looking happy and letting herself go. At that moment, she reminded me of Phorn and I started to feel rather uneasy about myself and my unplanned relationship with two young women instead of only one. I was saying to myself that it was all an accident, it was all a coincidence. I had not planned it as I could not control what happened. With Pafua, it seemed emotional and tender love that I had to give before it would be returned, while with Phorn it was all emotional and physical giving on her part. It was not as if one was complementing the other, as they were similar in some ways yet very different in others. I did not know why but when I was with one, I hardly thought of the other.

I did not want this thought to spoil my afternoon with Pafua, so I kept on taking photographs of her looking at the fish, sitting on the concrete edge of the pond in the park, or standing in front of some colorful flowers. Sometimes, she would ask if she could take my pictures and we would take turn with the camera, but it was mostly me taking her photos. We were the only people in the park, so we could not ask anyone to take photos of the two of us together. After a while, we went to sit on a public bench to give our feet some rest. I was sitting very close to her, and I felt again like putting my arms around her in this deserted park, but she said that people might see us and it would not look good so I was just looking at her and talking to her. We chatted for a few minutes about what she wanted to buy to bring back to her family in the refugee camp. She said she did not want me to spend too much money on them, and I said that we should buy them some foodstuffs and fruit, maybe a pair of shoes for her mother, sweets for her brother and a shirt for her sister.

"If you like, but you are spoiling them," she observed.

"No, I am happy to do it for you, because I want to show you how much I care for you and want to do things for you and your family."

"That's very nice of you, but don't spend too much money on us," she said, teasing me with a broad smile.

It was the first time we were by ourselves, feeling free to say what we liked. It was also one of the few times I saw her smile and not holding back, not hiding behind some wall in front of her mother. We were feeling really happy being there in that park with nobody around, as if in a world of our own. I loved looking at her smiling. It made her whole face and personality brighten up considerably like a dark room being suddenly illuminated by a white shining light. When at home in the refugee camp, she appeared to be restrained in her manners and did not seem to be able to relax, especially with her mother around us.

After we left the park, we walked to the market we were looking at from the hotel window earlier in the morning. We were wandering among the stalls and ended up in the food hall. Pafua wanted to have lunch there, but I said that it was rather smelly and looked unclean. She told me that was what made the food taste nice, so I did not make any more protest and we ordered fried noodle, steamed chicken and rice. We had to finish in a hurry because we had many things to do before catching the last bus back to Ban Vinai that afternoon. I looked at my watch, and it was only 12, still enough time for us to go and see a movie as Pafua said that she never missed going to the movies if she had the opportunity. It would also give us the chance to cool down after being at the park.

We went to the old movie house that I took her and her friends to the first time I visited her a few months ago. In those days, they only showed one movie at a time, and on that day it was a Chinese musical called "Love in the Pink Pavilion" with voice-over in Thai. We again went to sit at the back of the theatre and bought lots of fruit and snacks to eat, but we hardly ate any of them. As soon as the movie started, I could see that we were going to need a lot of tissues. The heroine was an orphan living with the hero's parents who have other marriage plans for him, and she spent much of the movie lamenting about the heart-breaking love she had for him, with her dying from pneumonia at the end just as her lover was getting married to the girl chosen by his family. After she died and he learned of her unrequited love, he left his wife to become a monk in the forest.

We were not even half way through the story when I noticed that Pafua was blowing her nose and wiping tears from her eyes with her handkerchief. I decided to comfort her and pulled her to me, feeling her crying silently. She did not make any sound, just letting the tears flow and wiping them away with her head on my shoulder. She made no resistance when I put my arm around her, and touched her tear-stained face with my other hand. I did not know why she should cry so much — just like Phorn when we went to our first Thai movie in Chiangmai. The two of them seemed to have something in common — they both loved sad movies and cried to them as if their own lives were full of sadness which no one could see and which they only showed in darkened movie houses. Or maybe they were only soft-hearted and kind with a lot of compassion for other people?

After the movie finished, we went again to the shops along the main street and then on to the market where we bought what we needed to take back to the refugee camp. It took us nearly an hour to finish the shopping, and we barely made it to the last bus. Pafua did not talk much after the crying session she had in the movie house, and I did not want to break her silent self-recollection as we were shopping, except to make the odd remarks about what we were buying and the quality of things we were looking at. On the bus, she was more talkative, and we chatted most of the way home when it was not too dusty so that you had to keep your mouth closed to avoid swallowing the dust raised by the old bus as it struggled its way slowly to Pakchom past Ban Vinai where we alighted. We were discussing the Chinese movie much of the time, and making comments about the end where the heroine died coughing blood and singing through her tears. Pafua agreed that it was a very sad love story, and she hoped that she would not go through something like that in real life. I said she should not worry about it, as it was only a story made up by someone.

Chapter 11

When we got back to Ban Vinai, I returned to Lychu's house in the evening after taking some food we had bought from Loei at Pafua's house. Her eyes were still red and puffy from the crying she did in the movie house, but she was not sad anymore — just her usual distant and proper self by the time we arrived at Ban Vinai. I was afraid that her mother might want to know about her swollen eyes, but I was glad that she did not say anything. For the first time, I had really tender and caring feelings for Pafua, and wanted to take care of her and be with her the rest of my life. I could not help thinking about her reactions to me in the hotel room, which were very different from those at the movie house. But I thought that maybe I should not make too much of them, that at least she did not resist my holding or touching her. What bothered me, though, was the fact that I might have offended her for trying to show her my physical affection, and she might start to dislike me thinking that I was taking advantage of her.

After we had finished dinner, Lychu asked me to sit with him under a tree outside his family's kitchen where a crude bamboo bench was set up for people to get some breeze when the sun became too hot during the day. He used to be a subsistence farmer in some distant village in the highlands of Xieng Khouang in northern Laos, but was conscripted into the Royal Lao Army during the push against North Vietnamese troops that came to invade Laos in violation of the 1962 Geneva Cease-fire Agreement. Many Hmong men did not accept this conscription, preferring to stay alive in their villages and carrying on with their subsistence farming. Some even ran away to be on the enemy side to avoid conscription. Lychu was one of those who did not resist being put into the army, and now found himself in the refugee camp with his four brothers and his elderly parents. He was a tall generous man, with skin darkened by the hot Thailand sun after he had to work whenever he could in local Thai farms to get food for his wife and seven children of varying ages.

Tonight, the temperature was very high with hardly any breeze under the tree outside Lychu's kitchen. As usual, other refugees were out playing or talking in front of their buildings. There was a lot of chatting and noise from people cooking or cleaning in their kitchens. Some were listening to Thai and Hmong broadcasts on their radio sets, and seemed to turn up the volume to its highest level as if to compete with each other. The lack of space, this myriad of noise and the stifling heat combined to exacerbate everyone's discomfort.

Lychu was fanning himself with a Thai newspaper when he turned and said to me, "I heard that you had come here to marry Pafua. Is that right?"

"Yes, but not straight away. We have to see how things work out."

After a brief pause during which he seemed to be thinking hard, he continued, "You know, we think highly of you. You are one of the very few Hmong who have gone to a Western country for education. We have great respect for you, but you should be careful."

I was curious. I did not know what he was referring to. I asked, "Tell me, what do you mean?"

"I mean Pafua and you. Since you came here, many people have been watching you to see if you will be doing things right. You'll have to be careful about what you say or do."

"Really? Why is that?"

"You have been away from us for many years. You may have forgotten some of our customs. Before you do something, talk to us first. We are your relatives and we are always ready to help you," he said.

"Yes, I will. And thank you for offering to help me. I will let you know when I need it," I replied.

The next day, I did not go immediately to pay my usual visit to Pafua and her mother. I was afraid I might say something wrong to them, after what Lychu had said to me. Instead, I went to see the leader of a Hmong messianic movement called "Chao Fa" (Lord of the Sky) which had been thriving in the camp for nearly a year and was said to have many followers. He lived in Section 2 of the camp on the other side of the hill beyond Pafua's house. A tall man for a Hmong, he told me about their version of the coming of a new world order and how the Hmong fitted in

God's scheme of things. I asked him how he knew these things, and he said the spirits came to deliver messages to him at night. He had high hope of the Hmong refugees returning to live in Laos because "God will intervene when the Hmong live in houses built on rocks and timber stilts." He proudly pointed at the long houses built by the Office of the UN High Commission for Refugees on concrete posts with the raised timber floor. I thought the whole thing was rather interesting, if not somewhat amusing.

On the way back from Section 2, I passed by Pafua's building but the doors were all closed. I asked the neighbors where she was, but they did not know. I was rather disappointed, but then I could not expect her to give me every minute of her time just because I was in the camp and hoping to marry her. I had not married her, so she still did not "belong" to me, as the Hmong would say. All the same, I often wondered where she could have gone every time I came and did not find her. I spent three more days at the camp and went to call on Pafua on three or four occasions, sometimes sharing a meal with her and her family. She always received me warmly and talked to me the way she had always done. I began to like her more and more, but I also felt sorry for her, with a mother, younger sister and brother to look after — in a refugee camp where there was no work and no land to grow anything for yourself but only masses of people and buildings everywhere surrounded by barbed wire and Thai soldiers. And every day, there was the sound of people wailing and music playing at funerals because so many refugees died from sickness and diseases.

Every square foot of the camp seemed to be used for something: houses, outside toilets, vegetable gardens, walk ways, or cemeteries. Apart from the school and a hospital, there was a market serving more than 40,000 refugees. There was not much at the market, except for a few shops selling noodle, meat and vegetables. The rest of the stalls sold handicrafts: wall hangings, pillow cases and bed spreads adorned with fine Hmong embroideries made by refugee women who had much time on their hands but no other means to make a living. Most of the refugees in the camp depended on the support of the United Nations, the Thai government and relatives living in other countries who would occasionally send them money so they could survive. There was a lot of sickness because of the over-crowding and lack of health care; many children and elderly people died every day and the cemeteries were filling quickly. Maybe some of the old people might have died from despair and the loss of hope of going back to a peaceful Laos or being accepted for settlement in another country.

I could not understand how Pafua and her family had managed to subsist in this oppressive place full of people and squalor everywhere you stepped into. The outside toilets were built in a row not far from each cluster of two or three main buildings, and you had to take your own water to wash and to have your own key to use the one allocated to your group. It was probably the best the UN could do under the circumstance, but they all looked and smelled rather unclean. And what had happened to her step-father whom she had never mentioned in our conversations? Sometimes, I felt rather guilty that I had been so much luckier than her and her mother. To make up for this, I asked Pafua to go with me to Pakchom on my last day in the camp. Pakchom was a sleepy little town, about five or six kilometers from Ban Vinai, perched on the bank of the Mekong River overlooking the border between Thailand and Laos. The border was actually an invisible line running the middle of the Mekong all the way from Sayabury Province in the north of Laos down to Pakse in the south near the Cambodian border.

We went there on the old bus that travelled between Loei and Pakchom going past the refugee camp, the bus which Pafua and I had taken a few times on our shopping trips to Loei. There were only a few Thai passengers on the bus, for it was near the end of its journey. It was making its clanky way along the dirt road with potholes and pools of yellow rain water here and there. Apart from the noise made by the bus engine when the driver tried to push it hard, there seemed to be no other sounds. Everything was quiet and a small breeze was blowing that seemed to make the heat more tolerable. There was not much to see or do in Pakchom. It had a small market with some stalls and shops, but most of the town had only little timber houses belonging to local farmers. It was really just another big farming village on the road linking Nongkhai to the south and Dansai further to the north in Phetchabun

Province. But it was the town closest to the camp, and many UN and non-government foreign refugee workers had their living quarters there. They travelled to work in Ban Vinai during the day and went back to Pakchom in the evening.

I took Pafua to lunch in a decrepit old restaurant built on a raised open timber deck a few meters from the muddy Mekong river. The river stretched across yellow water and mud embankments and you could see thick lines of green bamboo trees along the other side in Laos with small grass houses in between them. Now and then, a boat would struggle up the river with its old engine spluttering and a flag at the hem to indicate whether it belonged to the Lao or the Thai side. The restaurant was deserted, and peaceful with a breeze blowing through its balustrades. The were no other sounds to break the slow pace of business in the place, apart from the cooking from the restaurant kitchen at the back of room and the engine sound of a car passing along the road not far from the restaurant or beeping on its horn.

While Pafua was sipping her iced coffee, I said, "You know, it has been a while since we met. I don't have much time in Thailand and I would like to take you to live with me in Chiangmai. That way, I would not miss you so much and have to come to the camp. Will you marry me?"

She looked suddenly shy as if caught off her guard.

"I don't know," she replied in a calm voice. "It may be too soon. You'll have to ask my mother. I'd like to be with you, but my mother also needs me. She's got no one else to depend on in the camp."

"We will send her money. She can look after herself. She will have to let you go some time," I tried to convince her.

"I am afraid I can't answer you. Only my mother can."

I was annoyed that she seemed to defer everything to her mother instead of deciding things for herself. I had come a long way at her asking, and she was now giving this very meek, non-committal answer to the most important question of my life, of our life together.

"Maybe it's too soon. I will give us more time and see. Alright?" I said, trying to sound as if I was only joking with her earlier when I seriously asked her to marry me.

I did not realize then the differences between us at that time — the cultural gulf that separated me and her. Like other people used to the individualistic, free life style in Western countries, I always liked to make my decisions by myself and to speak my own mind. Like other well brought-up Asian young girls, Pafua was trying to do the right thing by being indecisive and modest, by saying little when it concerned her life and leaving the major decisions on herself to the family, the kin group and to her mother. For these young women, the family had the over-riding authority over the individual, although the latter was consulted on matters that concerned him or her. I was becoming rather impatient and found her old-fashioned attitudes frustrating. I was wishing that she could talk more openly and make her own decisions, so that I would not have to go back and forth between my work at Chiangmai and the refugee camp many provinces apart. As usual, I would have to be patient and time might help to sort things out the way we wanted, for between now and the end of my stay in Thailand anything could happen. We might come to understand each other better, and to be able to decide things for ourselves.

Chapter 12

Before I left Pafua to return to Chiangmai, I gave her 3,000 Baht and said I would send her more after I got back to Chiangmai and got money from the bank. She did not accept it readily, like all good-mannered and well-bred Hmong; you were supposed to refuse even if you wanted to have it. I gave her the money, because I felt a sense of real love and concern for her. Yet, after all I had done, why did she refuse my marriage proposal? I kept wondering. I decided that I would give our relationship more time before I asked her mother for her hands as she suggested. I would send her more money to convince her that I really wanted her. I could afford to do it with my payment of $600 a month from the University of Minnesota, and that translated into a lot of money in Thailand, especially for me who was living a moderate and simple life like one of the locals and not a Farang. Although I knew something about Hmong courting practices, I was also determined to know more about the Hmong culture and do things right with Pafua, so I decided to ask the Hmong at Maewang about their courtship and marriage customs.

After I returned to the Hmong village, I went to see Zong Cheng, the village headman. Many Hmong men in the village got married by asking their wives directly after a period of courtship, but I wanted to know whether there were other ways. It was said that sometimes girls were kidnapped by prospective husbands, or some might be forced to marry men who came to ask for their hands with their parents because the men might be rich or prominent people in the community. Some men married two or three wives in this way, often against the wishes of their first wives. There were only two or three polygamous marriages in Maewang. Zong Cheng himself only had one wife. I did not tell him what happened between me and Pafua at Ban Vinai.

It was early in the evening as we were chatting around his smoky fireplace. I asked him, "Uncle, sometimes a girl may show that she loves you, but may not agree to marry you. Does that happen, and what should the man do?"

"Yes, it does happen but that would be very rare. Normally if you love each other, the girl will just come home with you so the two of you can get married. All you have to do in that case is to send messengers to tell her parents that she is with you and to fix a wedding date. The Hmong call this *"fi xov"* (fi sor) or informing the girl's parents of her whereabouts. If you don't do the *fi xov*, the parents may get worried about their daughter gone missing, and they will impose a big fine when you come to have the wedding ceremony," he kindly explained.

"I see, but what would you do if the girl does not want to run away with you? She loves you, but she keeps saying you should ask her parents to see if they will let her marry you. She would not answer you herself," I asked him further.

"If she acts that way, you have two choices. One is to kidnap her with the help of some friends and take her home by force, as it were. Once safely inside your house, and your elders have done the *lwm qaib* (lu kai) or acceptance ceremony using a rooster to put a ring around both your heads at the entrance to your house, she is yours. Her parents cannot take her back once she has undergone that ceremony; she is no longer part of their spiritual household because your family has accepted her into yours, even if this is against her will. A second choice for you is to formally ask for her hand with her parents. This is the better way, but it also means that the girl is too proud and wants to save face *tau ntsej muag* (tau je mua) in order to maintain respect for herself and her family by forcing you to have a *hais poj niam* (hay po nia) or wife-seeking ceremony. In this case, it means that she does not like you enough to run away with you, and you have to beg for her from her family. If she really loves you, a girl will usually just *khiav mus yuav txiv* (khia mu yua txi) or run off to get married with you."

"I see. But isn't there some contradiction in these customs? A girl can accept your marriage proposal herself, or you can ask for her from her parents?" I asked.

"No, there is no contradiction. They are just different choices young people can make."

"I would like to thank you warmly, Uncle. You have explained everything clearly and now I understand," I said, thinking about Pafua and her preferred approach to getting married.

According to Hmong customs, then, this would mean that she did not love me enough to accept my marriage proposal by herself, or else she wanted a formal proposal with her family so that I would give her more respect. But then, I said to myself, this might not necessarily be the case. She was not an ordinary Hmong girl with ordinary Hmong parents living in a village in the remote highlands of some country. Her parents were not peasant farmers like most Hmong were. Her father was a respected government official, and her family had always lived in the city. She was different. Now she had become a refugee with no home and I did not have a home in the refugee camp, too. Where would we go if she agreed to "run away" with me? To Lychu's house in Ban Vinai, or all the way to Chiangmai where I did not have any relatives to give her the acceptance ceremony? Maybe she had thought about all these problems and decided that there was no other way for us. Or maybe, she really did not like me enough and tried to give me hints about it?

I also wanted to experience the Hmong way of chatting up girls rather than just hearing people telling me about it, so the next day I asked Lue, one of the young men in the village, if I could go with him when he went *deev hluas nkauj* (deng lua gau) or courting at the small settlement up the river. I told him that although I was Hmong, I had never done this in my life, because I was always studying in foreign places and had had no opportunity to live a real Hmong life. He asked whether I knew how to play the Hmong *ncas* or mouth harp musical instrument, or the long flute. Both of them were often used by young men outside a girl's bedroom at night to attract her attention. I said that I did not know how to play any of these musical instruments, but expected him to play them for me when we went courting. He laughed and said he would be happy to show me how things were done.

After Lue finished his farm work that day, we had dinner at the UN compound where I was based, then set off to his girlfriend's village about two kilometers upstream. He told me that there were two other single young girls there. I said I only wanted to see how he did his courting but that I did not want to do it myself because I did not know how to do it. He said that would be fine. We started after dark, using a torch each to see our way along the dirt walking trail that was full of holes and little rocks. We were each carrying a small blanket to keep warm, according to Lue. We had to choose our steps carefully as one minute you could be on level ground, then fall into a hole with your next step. Lue was used to the trail since he had been using it nearly every night. It was me who had the most trouble trying to catch up with him and to maintain steady steps in the darkness.

It was pitch black, and insects of all kinds were singing in the night from the bush and trees that surrounded the trail. The worst thing for me was that we had to go past the village cemetery and I always felt uncomfortable near cemeteries at night. As we were nearing it, I asked Lue if I could walk in front.

"What's the problem? Are you scared?" he asked.

"No, why should I? I am a grown-up man just like you," I pretended to put up a meek protest.

"Then just keep walking behind me," he joked.

"No way," I said, jumping in front of him as we went past a few old dirt graves just a few meters from the trail.

In the dark, it felt really spooky walking past the cemetery. I did not know how Lue could do it on his own every night going to see his girl and walking along this lonely track at night. I would not have risked doing it, even if the girl was Miss Universe. It felt rather daunting to me with the cemetery between the two villages. It just did not feel right that young Hmong people should only have time to court each other at night. But then again, there must be a lot of truth in the old Hmong saying: *"niam txiv txib ces mob mob, kev nraug txib ces khiav nce toj qob; niam txiv txib ces nkees nkees, kev nraug txib ces khiav nce toj qees"* (parents call and young men pretend to be frail, love calls and young men climb the steepest trail; parents call and young men pretend to be tired, love calls and young men brave a trail like fire).

As we were approaching his girlfriend's village, I asked Lue, "Why do Hmong do courting in the dark? Are they too shy to be seen by the girl's parents? Or is it because they are too busy with farming during the day?"

"It's all of that, and more. You will see," he pointed out.

It must be about eight when we arrived at the upper village. There were only six houses there, and some of the people were still up threshing rice and corn outside on the corn crusher, or working inside with the women doing embroideries by the light of the family fire or chopping pig feed from banana trunks. The older men were sitting around the fire smoking tobacco from their bongs, and the young boys attending the UN school were studying at the family dinner tables using candles for light. We did not go into any of houses, as we were not supposed to be seen by anyone. That seemed to be the rule, that young men doing courting should not allow themselves to be seen openly, even in the dark, otherwise it would be seen as a sign of disrespect and lack of good manners.

Lue said that we were too early and had to wait until the old people went to bed, then their daughters would follow and when everything was quiet, we could home in. We were standing at the entrance to the village, and dogs were barking non-stop at us. We had to speak in whispers.

"What do you mean by homing in?" I asked Lue.

"I will show you," he said.

I felt very uncomfortable, hiding behind the cover of a large bush in the dark and being barked at by all the village dogs as if we were bandits getting ready to swoop in on some innocent villagers. But Lue was just standing there as if it was the most natural thing to do, not minding in the least that mosquitoes were biting us all over the place, on our exposed arms and our faces. After about half an hour, the fires inside the houses went out one by one, as people were turning in. Lue motioned me to go into the village with him, inviting a new round of barking from the dogs. It was good that they were happy just barking at us, instead of running to us to find something to get their teeth into. They must have got used to seeing Lue and knew him by sight, but maybe were barking only at me as a first-time night visitor to their village.

Lue went to crouch outside the southern wall of one of the houses where his girlfriend's bedroom was apparently located. He then got out his mouth harp, and started blowing some muffled musical notes that served as love message through one of the gaps into the timber boards of the wall separating him and the young girl's bed. By now the dogs had stopped barking and seemed to think that we were just a waste of time because we were not doing any harm to the village, just two young men trying to court the village girls like they had seen a thousand times before. Lue continued to play his harp music for a good two to three minutes, then whispered into the gap, calling the girl's name. The girl on the bed inside soon whispered back and they started a love conversation that went in whispers for the next five minutes, all the while he was still crouching outside the wall. I was crouching alongside him, trying to listen to what they were saying to each other, but I also felt like I was intruding into their private world. At any rate, I did not hear them clearly enough half the time to make out what they were saying to each other.

After a while I felt rather awkward and uncomfortable crouching there next to him, not knowing what to do and with no girl to talk in whispers to. He gave me a nudge and whispered that it was now my turn to give it a try. I told him ever so softly that I could not do it because she was his girlfriend, but he said that she was not his and that I should feel free to whisper anything I like to her. I asked him what should I say to the girl, and he suggested that I should just say anything that came to mind, like asking her if she liked me or not. I told him I could not do that, she did not know me. He said not to worry, it was just for fun, and if she liked me she would respond to my love calls, but I had to keep trying and not give up easily.

"You stay here with this girl, and I am going to chat up my real girlfriend at the next house. OK?" he said softly to my ears.

Before I could say anything back to him, he was gone into the darkness and I did not know which house he had scurried to. I was left there by myself, outside this girl's bedroom in the dark, and I did not even know her name. I tried to put on a brave front and crouched down under the eve of the house, putting my mouth in the gap in the wall and called the young woman in whispers, asking her for her name and invited her to talk with me. By then, she must have realized that the guy outside was too green and inexperienced, and she just would not whisper back to me, no matter how much I talked to her through the gap in the wall. It was as if everything seemed to have stopped and gone quiet all of a sudden in the village when the girl brought my courting game to a halt. Lue had told me earlier that if a girl pretended to be asleep, the young man could attract her attention with a little stick. A little dry bamboo stalk happened to be near my feet, and I put it into the wall gap to try to rouse the girl by touching her with it, but she pretended to be fast asleep. I shone the torch light in, and I touched her hair and I touched her arm with the bamboo stick, but nothing happened. I soon gave up in frustration, and went looking for Lue, but found him nowhere. I went around all the other houses, shining my torch in front of me so I would not trip over some objects and make a terrible noise. Lue was not outside any of them.

I did not know where he would have gone; maybe his girlfriend had let him inside her bedroom to sleep with her, or maybe she had come out and they had gone into the bush. This seemed to be what happened when two young people were really in love and intent to get married. They played a more intimate game this way. That is why young Hmong do courting at night, so nobody can see them. I did not know how I could find Lue and where else to look for him. I would not know where to go scouting around the bush that surrounded the village to find him; and in any case I would not want to intrude or to interrupt whatever he was doing with his girlfriend. In the end, I just went into a horse stable and stayed among the horses there to keep myself warm and to have company. I was rather scared being by myself roaming aimlessly in the village in the dark.

The cemetery and all the ghost movies I had seen in America came flashing back in my mind. I put the blanket over me and covered myself from head to foot, hiding in it sitting on the dirt and leaning against a post outside the horse stable. I was also concerned that someone would come out and find me, the educated Hmong extension worker from America whom everyone looked up so much to. But I could not do anything much at that moment. I couldn't knock on somebody's door and ask to stay for the night. That was not what Hmong young men courting were supposed to do. On the other hand, I could not return to the lower village by myself, not with the cemetery I had to pass on the way in the darkness of the night. So I just stayed there inside my blanket, listening to the horses moving in the stable and putting up with the big stench from the horse droppings and urine around me.

I must have dozed off, I did not know for how long. The horses had gone quiet when I was woken up by Lue. He said that it was getting late and that we should head down back home. I asked him what was the time, rubbing my sleepy eyes. He replied that it was one o'clock in the morning. After we left the village and could talk at normal conversation level, I asked him as we were walking back under the torch light, "How did you find me? Did you know I was sleeping at the horse stable?"

"Well, it took me a while to look, but I eventually found you."

"Where did you go all night? I couldn't find you anywhere after you left. The girl did not like me and just would not talk to me," I said, sounding upset and trying to put the blame on him.

"Is that right? I thought I should leave you to have a good time with her."

"Well, it's you who had the good time, not me. As I said, the girl didn't talk to me. Maybe she recognized me, or maybe I said the wrong things to her? Where did you disappear to, anyway?"

"We went to the bush," he said casually as if there was nothing exciting or wrong about it.

"I was trying to look for you everywhere, but couldn't find you. Anyway, I didn't want to invade your privacy, so I went to stay with the horses," I said.

"Well, there is no such thing as privacy in Hmong culture. We all usually share in the fun. But we went a rather long way to our favorite spot. You wouldn't be able to find us," he explained.

"May I ask what were you doing there?" I teased him

"Not much. We were just having fun. She usually comes out and goes with me to the bush where we can talk more comfortably."

"Usually, Hmong girls just come out of their houses at night to play courting games with boys?" I asked.

"Yes, once you get to know them well. It's just fun most of the time, without them thinking about marriage necessarily."

"And these outdoor games in the bush in the dark, what are they?"

"Well, that's when the blanket comes in handy. You usually just wrap it around you and the girl to protect from the cold and the mosquitoes, but really so you can feel her as you talk the night away."

"What, she let you feel her anywhere?"

"Well. Almost. It depends on her, how far she will let you."

"I hear that premarital sex is not allowed in Hmong society, but it seems to be fairly common among young Hmong people. With all this game-playing in the bush, don't you do more than feeling and petting?" I asked him.

"It again depends on the girl. Some would go all the way, but others would just let you feel. Most Hmong men prefer their real wives to be virgins, but some don't care."

"Doesn't that mean some Hmong girls may get pregnant before marriage?"

"Yes, some do. If that happens, the boy will have to marry the girl involved. If she cannot identify the baby's father, then she ends up with no one and is then seen as trash, easy game for men," Lue explained in between overstepping some boulders along the trail.

"That's sad. Don't Hmong people use birth control, I mean things people do to stop girls from getting pregnant?"

"No, we don't know. Not like other people in other places. What about you, what do you do?" he asked, suddenly catching me off-guard.

"Oh! I don't know. I know what Western people do. I read in books, but I have not used any of these ideas myself. They take pills, and do many other things."

The conversation had become rather personal and I was embarrassed. I did not want him to think that I was still a virgin when most village young people started this side of life at around 16 years of age. We changed the conversation to other things, to life in America and how young Americans did their courting. We talked so much that we arrived back at the main village without me realizing. We had long passed the cemetery along the way and I had not felt scared at all. Nothing much happened that night, but I had learned a lot. I had also learned that this kind of night game-playing between Hmong young people was not something I would like to do. I preferred a more indiscreet direct approach in front of the girl's family when I wanted to talk to her, as I had done with Pafua in Ban Vinai although that might not be the Hmong way. I really did not want to brave the cold, barking dogs in the darkness, smelly horse droppings, mosquitoes and spooky feelings as you stumbled past cemeteries by yourself just so that you could talk in whisper with a girl at the end of your night journey and then had to return home to have some sleep and get up early for the next day's work. No, that was not for me. I preferred chatting normally, looking at the girl's face in the light and not her outside bedroom wall in the dark.

Chapter 13

After a few weeks of work in Maewang, I again went back to see Pafua at Ban Vinai. I was eager to test out what I had learned from the villagers about Hmong courtship and to try to really get a better idea on her true feelings for me. I took her an embroidered headband which I bought from a Hmong trader couple in a nearby village. It did not cost much, but I thought at least it would be something tangible from me that she could keep even though she might never use it, for such headbands were only used by the Hmong of Thailand.

The day after my arrival in the refugee camp, Pafua's mother told me that many Hmong in Ban Vinai had visited Hmong villages in various parts of Thailand, some making regular trips to sell herbal medicine and Hmong embroideries — sometimes even without official authorization. She said that she had heard so much about the Thai Hmong, but had never seen them. I asked whether she and Pafua would like to go and see a Hmong village. As I only had about a week off from work, I suggested that we could go to the closest Hmong settlement at Khek Noi in Phetchaboon Province, between Chumpae and Phitsanouloke, about a day away by bus from the camp. I knew the head man there well and had stayed at his house once on my way to Ban Vinai. His family was very hospitable and always welcomed guests to the settlement.

I went to obtain permission from the camp commander, and the three of us set off for Khek Noi the next day. Pafua had been to Bangkok and two or three other cities in northeast Thailand, but had not been to a Hmong village and was very excited at the prospect of visiting real traditional Hmong people. I was also looking forward to spending a few days in her company, although her mother would also be coming along. This would allow us to spend a longer time together than before when we could only have a few hours together.

On the bus to Loei, Pafua was sitting with her mother on a row of seats in front of me. I was contented with sharing a seat with a Thai man. I did not think much of it, as the old bus was only equipped with shared seats arranged in rows along either side of the bus interior. I would rather that she sat with her mother than have her mother sitting next to a stranger. She might also feel shy about sitting with me in the presence of her mother. When we changed to a bigger bus from Loei to Chumpae on which some of the shared seats could be occupied by three passengers, we all moved to one seat and she came to sit next to me. It was hot and rather dusty as usual. The noisy bus was crawling its way along the bumpy Thai country roads until we arrived in the late afternoon in Chumpae where I went to inquire and found that a Chiangmai bus was due to arrive from Khornkaen in a few minutes. This would get us to Khek Noi before midnight, but this would be better than spending the night at a hotel and getting a new bus the next morning. I bought tickets for the three of us for Khek Noi, and we soon boarded the Khornkaen bus as it docked at the bus bay. There were many people on this bus, and some were standing with no seats. We had to stand for quite a long way until the bus had passed a few Thai settlements and some people got off. Even then, we had to sit in different parts of the bus, as there were no vacant seats that the three of us could use and be together.

When we arrived at Khek Noi, it was nearly 11 o'clock at night. In those days, Khek Noi was a Hmong settlement of about 5,000 people, mostly evacuees from the so-called "Red Meo" war which staked Chinese-supported Hmong communist dissidents against the Royal Thai Army. The settlement was about half a kilometer from the main road linking Lomsak and Phisanouloke, and we had to walk the distance in the dark as there was no electricity in the area at that time. We did not bring any torches with us, but fortunately there were a few Hmong who got off the bus and were walking with us. We did not have much luggage, except for a small bag of personal possessions each. There were a lot of potholes on the dirt road leading to the settlement, and we had to carefully sift our way through without falling. Both sides of the road were lined with long blady grass, and crickets chirped into the night.

The headman, Zong Tua, was still up with his two wives and was talking to some villagers when we knocked on his door. He asked us inside, and straight away Pafua's mother fell into a long discussion with his two wives about life in the settlement. I said to him that we wanted to pay a visit to the settlement and asked him if we could stay at his house. I also told him what Pafua and her mother were with me. He said that we would be most welcome, and informed one of the wives to make a bed in his mother's room for them while I would sleep on the floor in the living room. It was cold but we each had a quick wash with cold water in the outside wash area next to the kitchen. After about an hour of chit-chatting with our hosts, we went to bed. It was late and we were tired from the bus trip. For some time, I could not go to sleep, thinking about Pafua who was sleeping not ten paces from me in another room. I wondered what she was thinking, how she found the exhausting bus ride and the arduous life of the Hmong which she would learn more about in the next few days.

It was May and the weather had began to cool after the rain season had set in. It was foggy in the morning. Heavy dew covered the grass along the trails to the fields so that you always got wet every time you had to go to the bush or to work on the family crops. Our guide told us that rice would be planted in July and be ready for harvesting by November when the Hmong would be busy cutting the yellowing rice stalks to leave them dry in the sun before the rice grains were threshed and transported home for storage. By then, most Hmong would also be occupied with the weeding of their opium fields which would continue until the New Year celebrations in December. Corn was usually grown in April as the first crop in opium poppy fields, but it was all harvested by July with the old corn plants cut and buried during the hoeing of the fields in preparation for the sowing of poppy seeds. Most of the fields nestled the slopes of steep hills or hidden away in narrow valleys around the Hmong settlement.

The next day after the morning dew that fed the grass overnight had dried in the late morning under the sunlight, Pafua asked if I could take her to visit the Hmong corn fields. She had seen rice fields only most of her life, but had not been to corn fields. We went to the nearest ones about three kilometers from the village. On the way, we were entertained by the sound of birds and cicadas singing in the woods. It was like taking a nostalgic journey back in time to search for your origin, going from village and civilization into the tree-covered jungles of Hmong ancestors in days that had long been gone. At the fields, you would hear more cicadas and other insects singing their hearts out from the surroundings, almost deafening your ears.

Pafua marvelled at the rich green corn plants with their lush long leaves, most of which were still too young to show any signs of cobs or even flowers. The corn plants were replaced by opium poppies in September and the poppy fields would be in full bloom by December with flowers of many colors ranging from pure white to blood red, and a mixture of red and white between. They were a beautiful sight to see, adorning the hill slopes, their sweet smell attracting bees and butterflies that flew slow and steady from one poppy flower to another, buzzing with concentration and drawing on the fragrance of the poppies to prolong their own survival. After the flowers dropped from the plants in January, the poppy pods would be mature enough for the farmers to make incisions with a small three-bladed knife from where the opium sap would ooze and be left to dry before being collected with a small thin knife. This opium harvest would take up most of January. By February, new fields would have to be cleared and a new farming and toiling cycle would start again for the following year. The daily grind of Hmong existence went on at this pace with one crop after another, day after day, repeating itself year after year.

During our visit, we saw the Hmong farmers weeding the corn fields by hand or with a small hoe, bending down and sometimes young wives carrying their small babies on their backs with a black apron. They would work from the early morning until lunch when they would stop, and resumed again after having their food which sometimes consisted only of rice and chili with little or nothing else. The chili helped chase the rice down your throat, as one of the Hmong women jokingly told us. She also said that the day's work would not finish until the sun went down and the women would start to collect pig feed from edible weeds or banana trunks that they would chop and cook that evening for the family pigs to eat the next morning. While the women collected feeds for pigs or grass for the family horses for the night, the men would collect firewood from the nearby trees if they needed to. They would usually return home as darkness settled around them.

The following morning, I took Pafua and her mother to visit Hmong families and the local market in Khek Noi. Although most of the Hmong here were still dependent on farming for their livelihood, a few who lived near the market had set up stalls outside their houses to sell groceries and other small goods. It was a small step to help supplement family incomes for those who could afford the manpower and capital that were needed for such trading activities.

In the afternoon, we went on foot to look at the waterfall north of Khek Noi and to take photographs with a few other young people Zong Toua had found to take us there. Pafua's mother said the trip would be too arduous for her, and decided to stay at the village. We walked for about an hour between corn fields before we reached the waterfall. The river was swift. Lush green vegetation and tall grasses were lining its two banks. The waterfall was very beautiful, with three levels of fast flowing jets of white water crashing onto rocks below — the last level emptying itself into a big green pond that looked deep and ominous. The Hmong believe that such ponds and lakes were often inhabited by dragons and evil spirits, and thus rarely ventured near them.

After taking some photos of ourselves there, Pafua and I went upstream to have lunch on a rock platform near the river bank, so we could admire the nice view from a safe distance. The other young people had gone further up the river for a walk. As we finished eating and were putting away our food, Pafua slipped from the rock and fell into the river. I was busy with the camera and could not stop her fall. In a matter of seconds, she was swept about 20 yards downstream. Luckily, the river was only waist-deep at this point and she was caught in a tree branch. Before realizing it, I had jumped into the river and made my way down towards her, even though I could not swim very well. After much effort, I managed to get her back on land. She was all wet, her blouse and skirt clinging to her body. She was shivering from the cold water, but put up a brave face by saying that it was nothing. I knew that her face betrayed her true feeling, for it showed how very frightened she was. Maybe, she just did not want me to see her in this state.

The currents were strong and she could have been washed down to the big green pond at the bottom of the fall. God only knows what would have happened then, as none of us was a very good swimmer. I put my arms around her waist and was hugging her to try to comfort her. Her breasts were touching me through her wet clothes. They were full, round and firm, very different from Phorn's soft, smaller ones. She had just had the fright of her life falling into the fast-flowing river and not knowing how to swim. It would not be right for me to do anything more than just hold her, although this was the first time that I felt her so intimately. Quickly however, she disengaged herself from me and hit my right arm with her small fist, saying that it would be embarrassing if the other young people there saw me cuddling her. She seemed suddenly shy and went back to sit on the rock with eyes downcast. She became quiet, refusing to look in my direction again. She looked so forlorn, like an orphan with no one to depend on. I must really love her, I said to myself. If she should die, it would mean not only the end for her mother, but also for me.

Later, we were sitting close to each other, looking down at the waterfalls and the tall trees with their green leaves lining the rocky banks of the river below.

"I am sorry I did not see you fall, so I could not stop it. You must be very afraid," I said to her.

"Yes, I was. But it was very sudden and I did not have much time to think."

"It really frightened me. I would not know what to do if something bad should happen to you," I continued, putting my fingers through a few strands of her soft, drying hair hanging down her back.

"Were you scared for me?" she asked.

"Yes, I was. I jumped into the water and I did not even think. It was like you are my very life and I was rescuing it from the dreadful clutches of the river."

"Really? You are very good — like you have always been. This is the second time you have saved my life. I really want to thank you for it," she said.

"When was the first time?" I teased her.

"When you sent money to me and decided to come to see me in Thailand."

"Yes, but I have not really finished my rescue yet."

"That doesn't matter. You have started the mission and that's all that counts," she teased back, making both of us laugh.

"Are you sure you did not fall into the river just now on purpose?" I continued to joke with her to make the most of our light conversation the way I often did with Phorn.

"Is that what you think?" she asked, and just bowed her head as if I had hurt her feelings.

Maybe she took life seriously and did not like to laugh at it. To change the subject, I said to her, "You know, I really love you, Pafua."

"Someone plain and with nothing like me, would you really love?" she asked the way Hmong girls usually did with their male courting partners.

"You are not plain. You are very beautiful and kind. You have a lot of courage. You asked me to come and help you. I love you for all that and more," I said.

When the other young Hmong returned from their walk, we immediately left the area and returned to Khek Noi. By the time we arrived, Pafua's clothes were almost dry from the heat and all the walking we had to do. When I told her mother what had happened, she was greatly alarmed, asking if we had done some soul-calling *"hu plig"* for her at the spot where she fell into the river. I told her that we were too afraid and forgot to do it, although in reality I did not know that such ritual would be needed. Even if I did, I would not know how to carry it out. She explained that when a person had a fall into the water, or was involved in a scary incident, the soul might become frightened and leave the body. This would result in the person getting sick and may even die if the soul was not brought back to the body through a soul-calling ceremony. This could be done by simply saying a few words to ask the soul to come back after the incident occurred. But if this was not done at the time, incense, paper money and a chicken would be needed so that its soul could be exchanged for the person's lost soul as the latter might have been captured by evil spirits after its flight from the body. I asked her if this was what we now had to do and she replied in the affirmative, but said that we had to wait until tomorrow.

Pafua protested that she was now a grown-up woman and was not scared from the accident at the river, but her mother wanted to ensure that she would not become sick. The next day, I went to buy a small chicken from the local market and we went back to the waterfall where a shaman was asked to perform the soul-calling ceremony. After reciting a long incantation urging Pafua's soul to return to her body, the shaman woman finished by asking the chicken for forgiveness and she gave it to Pafua to kill and steam it over a fire in a pot we had brought with us. When the chicken was cooked, she recited the incantation a second time. We then used the chicken meat for lunch and returned to the Khek Noi. Her mother seemed pleased, and I could see that Pafua also felt much relieved. Perhaps, that was what these Hmong ceremonies did to people — make them feel wanted and loved. The incident made me realize for the first time that her mother not only depended a lot on her but also loved her very deeply and did not want anything untoward to happen to her oldest daughter.

We stayed at Khek Noi two more days, then left to return to our separate destinations. I went on by bus to Chiangmai and Pafua and her mother travelled back to Ban Vinai on their own. I had no time left, so I did not go back there with them and they understood my situation.

Chapter 14

Now that I had come to know Pafua so well and let her know about my feelings, I decided to go to Bangkok after a month's work at Maewang. I wanted to consult the people at the American Embassy on how I could get married to Pafua and have her return to the US with me. I had not seen Phorn after I got back from Khek Noi, but went straight to the Hmong village where my Thai counterpart was continuing his work. He was starting to learn to speak Hmong, as he was going to be one of the experts on Hmong agriculture at the Tribal Development Center. At the time, there were very few educated young Hmong in Thailand, with hardly anyone reaching university level, so most of the public servants working with and for the Hmong and other hill tribes were lowland Thai people. There seemed to be no communication problem between them since many hill people spoke northern Thai well and could easily understand central Thai officials.

I still kept my lodging at Khun Samanh's house. After I left Maewang, I went to spend the night there before going to Bangkok at dawn the next morning. For the trip, I booked one of those expensive coaches that had air-conditioning and seats you could tilt back like those in the big commercial jetliners. Unlike the seats on the airplanes, however, passengers just sat anywhere they liked. I took a seat in the middle near the window to be safe in case of an accident, given that bus drivers in Thailand often acted like they were driving race cars rather than big heavy vehicles with many people on board. I was early and the coach was still waiting for other passengers, so I started to read a Thai newspaper I bought in the street earlier.

The next thing I knew someone was sitting in the seat next to me, put a small bag on the floor, then leaned lightly on my shoulder. I was startled by this act of familiarity, and looked. There was Phorn in her usual happy mood and breezy style — she seemed to just glide into any situation. I had not seen her for four weeks. She had on a pair of black jeans matched with a light blue silky shirt. Her long black hair was now cropped short, almost like that of a man. It made her look more mature, as if she had changed from a girl to a grown woman during the time that we had not been with each other.

I said to her, "You little devil, what do you think you're doing?"

"And what do you think I am doing?" she retorted, giving me a most disarming smile.

"Saying goodbye to me?"

"No, more than that. I am going to Bangkok."

"Doing business, I suppose?" I said rather teasingly like we often did to each other.

"No, to enjoy myself."

In our dalliances with each other before, I had never asked her if she had travelled anywhere. I did not know if she was familiar with the big city in the south.

"You have been there before?"

"Not really."

I was somewhat alarmed, but then this woman was always a big tease.

"What do you mean, you don't know Bangkok and you are going there? It's a big, big city with ten million people."

"Well, I am going with you, so why should I be scared? I am sure you will take good care of me," she said, full of confidence.

"You are so good at forcing yourself on me. This is the second time you have done it. Do you know that? Do you do this with other men, too?"

She looked suddenly crest-fallen and was near tears — like that time we were in the hotel bar many weeks before. Why did this woman affect me this way, I was asking myself? She always seemed to know how to make me do what she wanted and got away with it. Now, she did not say anything, but just stared past me at the people outside the bus window. I felt ashamed about what I had just said to her, after all the fun we had together during the last few months.

"OK, I was only kidding," I said. "I am glad you are coming. I will show you a good time in Bangkok. There are lots and lots of things to do and see."

"That sounds great. I can't wait for us to get there," she said, her bright eyes and cheerfulness slowly coming back.

I really did not want to go to Bangkok and be seen in the company of another woman. I had vowed to myself that I would be a good boy and tried not to hurt Pafua. I had by then decided that no matter what might happen, I was going to marry her to get her away from the over-crowded, dirty refugee camp and from a life of deprivation and without future. And I would try to give her all the things she did not have as a child, as an orphan whose father died before she was born, as a young girl who had to shoulder many family responsibilities. I would do everything to make her happy and forget all the bad times of the past. I would give her roses to adorn her life, to perfume her days and love would keep us side by side together to the end. But now Phorn was sitting in the bus beside me and I did not do anything. What could I do?

The bus was starting to move and people were saying goodbye to each other. I turned to Phorn and asked, "How did you know I would be on the bus?"

"Samanh told me last night, so I decided that I would surprise you after what you did to me. You have avoided me since you came back from Loei. What were you doing there?"

"Visiting friends," I replied.

"What kind of friends?"

"It's a secret I don't want you to know."

"You are being cruel again," she pointed out, looking away from me.

"Well, just relatives and people I used to know when I was a young boy in Laos," I said.

I went on to tell her about the Hmong on the Royal Lao government side, how they had fought against the communist Pathet Lao with the help of the American CIA but had lost the war, and thousands of them were now crowded together in three refugee camps across Thailand near the Lao border, with many more still stranded in Laos while a few had already gone to resettle in Western countries such as America, France, Canada and Australia. I told her that the refugees were a big burden on the Thai government, but the Thai people had been very understanding and helped many refugees crossing the Mekong river into Thailand. But many Hmong had drowned in the muddy water of this big river because they could not swim and because some evil-minded Thai boat owners tipped their boats to drown the refugees on board so that they could keep their luggage and other valuable possessions.

Phorn was rather shocked and said that she had never heard of refugees coming from Laos, and asked if she could go to the refugee camp with me next time I went there.

"It's very hard to get into the camp, and you would be very bored because the people there don't speak Thai," I said.

I was trying to discourage her from the idea, not wanting her to come along on my next visit to see Pafua. I did not want to start a battle between the two women in my life at the time, since I would myself more than likely end up being the refugee from the fight between them.

"That's no problem, I would be with you. You speak perfect Thai and you can be my interpreter," Phorn announced as if nothing would ever bother her when she was with me.

"We will see, alright?" I said, not wishing to hurt her feelings but making no promises.

She seemed to be forever optimistic, with a solution to every little situation. To me, she was generous to a fault, always curious and forever giving of herself. She did not seem to ask for anything in return, and was often after some fun and a good laugh. I had never told her about Pafua, and I certainly did not want Pafua to know about my association with Phorn. I only hoped that things would sort themselves out in the end, somehow. I sometimes found it hard to read other people, and I suspected that Phorn's cheerfulness on the outside might just be a cover-up for some deep hurt inside that frail, little frame. She was running after "a good time" at every opportunity as she proudly proclaimed, but now and then her eyes were also brimming with silent tears. I had not tried to find out why she showed this contradiction in her otherwise seemingly happy life, because I did not want to cause her any needless pain.

By the time we arrived at Lampang, the next provincial city on our route, Phorn was already asleep. She was sitting in the inside bus seat, leaning her head on my right shoulder as if it was a familiar habit, a most convenient thing for her to do. I tried to wake her up a few times so she could see the beautiful Thai countryside, the busy traffic and the little villages we were passing through. But she did not seem to be interested. She said she would rather go to sleep to avoid getting car sick, so I let her be. All the way to Bangkok, she only woke up when we stopped for lunch at Phitsanuloke or for refreshments and going to the toilet at a few other stops.

It was an all-day journey. We arrived on Sunday night and went to stay in a medium class hotel in Saphankhuai after we left the bus. The hotel was called the Washington. Phorn had been living long enough in Chiangmai city to act like a real city person, and she never showed that she was a country girl. It was a long way from Silom where the American Embassy was located, but it was the part of Bangkok I was most familiar with. It was not very posh and many of the buildings were old with no big shopping malls, but it had many small stalls and shops selling all kinds of things. It was also a more peaceful part of Bangkok. Anyone who had been to the City of Angels, as Bangkok is also known, would have their senses knocked about in all directions. Like in all big cities of the world, the sight of the slow traffic, the smell of open and untreated sewerage, the noise of cars combined with the unrelenting heat were most obtrusive. They seemed to hit you all of a sudden as you got out of the airport into the street or out of long-distance buses from the outer provinces. This seemed to be particularly the case on a first visit. After a while, you came to get used to them and hardly noticed anything while you went about your business.

After a shower at the hotel, we went for dinner at a night market along one of the main busy streets with the usual evening traffic flowing through more briskly than during the day, but the cars were still beeping on their eternal horns. We then took a short walk around the block, but most of the shops were closed so we returned to the hotel for an early night. I was wondering what would be in store for Phorn and me, this being the second time we were together by ourselves in a hotel room.

However, I was rather exhausted from the long bus trip, and Phorn said she had a headache as well. We went to sleep in one of the twin beds in the room, as we could not find one with a double bed. It was just big enough for us to fit in snugly. As usual, it was hot and we left the air-conditioner on all night. It helped cool down the heat in the room and also muffled the street noise.

Chapter 15

In the morning, Phorn was very sick with a high fever and a runny nose. She had come down with a cold or something. She was sweating and could not get up. Because of the hot weather, we had been sleeping without much clothing on, and during the night she must have kicked off the blanket on her side of the bed. She must have been exposed to the cold air from the air-conditioner during most of the night, and became more ill from the headache she had complained about the previous evening.

She was shivering with fever and her teeth were chattering. Her nose was blocked and she spoke in a very nasal voice like the famous movie star, Audrey Hepburn, in some of her funny movies. I was really worried that it would be more than just a cold, maybe some kind of horrible fever people have been heard to have died from within a few hours. If she died while we were in Bangkok, that would be terrible as I would not know what to do. I knew nothing about her family or friends. I said to myself that she could not die, and that I must not think about death. It might just be a really bad cold, and she would recover soon.

I did not know who to contact. I rang the hotel reception and ask if they could get us a doctor. They said there was a clinic nearby where we could just get to by taxi. I told them that Phorn could not get up from bed to come down and catch a taxi. They suggested that she try, as there was no ambulance they could get. I did not know what best to do, so I said I would see what we could do. I tried to get her up but she could not move. I put some clothes on her the best way I could. She was complaining of feeling cold, but she felt hot like a burning fire. She kept saying that it was nothing and that she would be alright soon. She refused to see a doctor or go to a hospital.

"Why, you need to get better so we can go and look at Bangkok. There are so many things to see, nice food to eat and fun things to do. I want you to really enjoy yourself, not getting sick," I said, trying to cheer her up.

"You are so nice. Why are you so nice?" she said, looking at me weakly from the bed.

I was bending down, touching her head and then her cheek slowly and tenderly. At that moment, I seemed to have forgotten all about Pafua and rescuing her from the refugee camp. All I wanted was to rescue Phorn from this terrible sickness and maybe even from death.

"I want you to get up so we can go to the hospital," I said softly.

"No, I can't go. I can't pay the hospital. I used my last money for the bus fare to come with you yesterday," she replied.

"What do you mean? That was less than two hundred Baht for a return ticket."

"That's all I had left from my last salary," she explained weakly.

"Don't talk, you are sick. I will take care of everything. I want you to recover and live for a long time," I said to comfort her.

"I want to live. I don't want to die. I can't die."

"Poor Phorn. Poor little Phorn, you won't die. You need to get well."

"I won't die. I have always recovered. Just get me some tablets, and I will be alright," she said motioning me to go out.

Her nose and her eyes were all running, and I passed her a roll of tissues I got from the bathroom. Her face was red, but she was trying to put on a brave face and smiled. She must also be hungry and needed some food. I told her to stay in bed, and went down the lift to ask where was the nearest drug store. In Thailand, you could get all kinds of medicine without prescription, and I wanted to get something to give to Phorn so she could get well enough for me to take her to a hospital. I dashed out of the hotel and walked into the main street, feeling depressed and lonely as I was hurrying to find a pharmacy. I suddenly felt, not like a white knight trying to rescue Phorn but more like a desperate man about to lose his soul mate to some evil power beyond my control.

When I got back to the hotel, she seemed to look better. I bought her some food so she could take before I gave her the medicine for the fever. I asked if she was hungry but she said no. Looking down at her small figure, I touched her on the forehead.

"Your face is so red with fever. I want you to eat. I want you to look beautiful the way you were before you got sick," I said to her.

"And you think I was beautiful?" she asked slowly.

"Yes, your little face was beautiful. Your small body was beautiful, and your big heart was too."

"Now you are joking. Now I am sick and I am not beautiful any more," she said.

"Stop talking and eat some food."

I fed her the soup that I bought from the stall in the street in front of the hotel. She did not want to eat, but I said she had to have food before taking her medicine. She took a few spoonfuls, then two cold and flu tablets with the water from the bottle I got her from the shop downstairs.

"Poor darling, I am such a burden on you," she said, lying on her side on the hotel bed.

She looked much better after the food and the medicine. I was washing her weak slender arms with a wet towel when I heard her say "darling" but I no longer cringed at it. The word seemed to fit the situation perfectly, although we had never talked about our feelings for each other before. We had enjoyed the rapture of our bodies and the pleasure of each other's company, but I had tried not to feel anything else as if there were no other cravings and no other feelings in our relationship. But at that moment, it did not seem to matter how she saw it.

"Get well. You will be beautiful and strong again, like you have always been," I said, wiping away at her face.

"Yes, I want to — for me and my child," she whispered in a forlorn voice.

I realized that she had just dropped a bombshell, but I did not want to show her my surprise, so I just asked her as gently as possible, "What child?"

"My daughter. I have a five-year old daughter living with my mother in the country. Only a few people know about her."

"But you have never told me you have a daughter," I said.

"Yes. I was married before, but got divorced three years ago."

"Why didn't you tell me this before?" I scolded her.

"I did not have time. And I did not know you well enough."

"And now you think you know me," I said, more a confirmation than a question to her.

"Yes, you are nice and kind. I can see it from what you have done for me. I can see it on your face. That's why I like you and can tell you about my life."

Now I understood why her eyes sometimes seemed to fill with tears, and she would always explain it by saying that she was only being silly. People always try to bear their heavy burdens in silence, to keep them as their deepest secrets and only talk about them at the right time and with people they feel something special with. Good people who have suffered deep hurts always deny themselves and go on giving to others to hide the pain and the suffering inside, to put on a good front. I was moved. No one had ever said anything like that to me, maybe from lack of chance encounters that forced me to share and to give, to become one with the other person.

I looked at Phorn and she was also staring at me with her loving eyes — all the gay abandon she usually displayed was gone and replaced with real tenderness — something she did not need to pretend to have and to use as a cover-up for the problems and the hurt in her young life. Without a word, I kissed her. Her nose was running and her eyes were running. And I kissed the tears away, tasting their saltiness running from her dark, beautiful eyes. At that moment, I lost all care for other things and other people. After a short time, she responded and turned to lie on her back, giving me her sweet lips, her little nose and her soft face. It was not the kissing of two people in the throes of animal lust that we had experienced at the expensive Lanna Hotel in Chiangmai, but of two people yielding and giving the deepest feelings they had for each other. I was touching her fevered and weak body, and she let my hand roam freely, looking at me tenderly as if to say that I should not hold back, for she was all for me to see, to touch, to protect and care for, to admire and enjoy.

After what seemed like a long time, her hands were roaming to the front of my shirt and down to the opening of my trousers. She was unzipping me, touching me, trying to give more of herself and to undress me even in her sickness, as if that was the ultimate thing I wanted from her that she could offer me, the culmination and the peak in this moment of tenderness.

"But you are sick. We still have other times," I whispered to her ear.

"Poor darling, always the right time and place for everything. Why must that be with love?" she said softly, still looking at me.

I did not seem to care that she had said the word "love." I did not know what I felt for her, whether it was love or pity, or my need to give and not just to take from her. I did not care how many other men might have slept with her. We had never talked about them, about whom we had slept with. It was neither her fault nor mine that we did not meet when she was younger and innocent, without a child and a divorce. At that moment, nothing seemed to matter. All I wanted then was to bath in the warmth of her hot body, in the fever of her sickness and the depth of her love that was hot and wet, pouring out like a fountain of thirst from the core of her tiny body, from her very life. She was crying and moaning softly, but not wailing, just crying silently with large drops of tears and sniffling through her blocked runny nose.

It was as if we were transported to a land of great joy while confined to a place of great pain. Our hearts were running holding hands with each other, throbbing in unison and singing songs of joy to their uncharted journey of discovery that seemed tainted also with a touch of despair. I was running along the journey as fast as I could, and when I got too far ahead of her I slowed down, waiting for her to catch up with me. The game went on and on until she came in waves after waves of happiness that squeezed me like a vice and at the same time caressing me like the perfumed petals of full-bloom roses. I reached for the nectar of life in her and it was given, without reserve or demand for anything in return, without mystery.

We went to sleep in that state of being suspended between life and death and yet never so happy. It was late in the afternoon before I woke up. Phorn was already sitting by the small table at the wall near the foot of the bed, and was brushing her short hair. She had already put on a flowery dress, as if waiting to go out. Her eyes and nose seemed to have stopped running.

"How are you feeling?" I asked her.

"Better. Much better," she replied in her sick Audrey Hepburn nasal voice that sounded so endearing and child-like.

I was amazed, thinking that maybe love really had healing powers, as people say. Being the skeptic that I always was, however, I put it down to just coincidence. But perhaps, it was more than that. I was wondering what Phorn was feeling at that moment, sitting there by the small table at the foot of our hotel bed, slowly brushing her short hair and adjusting her green flowery dress. She looked lovely, innocent and all confident again. She did not say anything, just brushing her hair and looking into the mirror, like she was content with her dream of love fulfilled and the picture of her beloved in her heart. I did not know what to feel, whether to be content like her or to worry about what to do with my problem of having two women, with each not knowing about the other but committing herself more and more to me as if she was my only relationship. I might have a song of praise for their love, but I was also suffocating from the knot I was tying myself into, from the fate of a young man who fell upon the love of more than one woman, the rescuing knight charging through in heavy armor but not knowing that there were two women instead of one waiting for his rescue at the end of his journey. Was I being selfish, or was I too naive and took on more than I could chew, I asked myself? But like Scarlet O'Hara in Margaret Mitchell's book *Gone with the Wind*, I shall think about my problem tomorrow, because today I have too many other things to do and my mind now only has room for nice kindly thoughts.

Chapter 16

We stayed in the hotel watching TV most of that day to give Phorn time to rest and recover from her sickness. There were only three or four TV channels on the set in the hotel room. Phorn wanted to watch some Thai soapies and I let her do it until we could not find anymore of them on any of the channels. Then I switched to some English and French broadcast. She was delighted that I could understand so many languages when she only had Thai and her northern dialect. She wanted to know where I had learned them. I told her that I learned some of them from schools in Laos, and some I learned by myself from reading and listening to the radio. She seemed to be very proud, and I was happy for her. I wanted her to get well so we could go out, do some sightseeing, finish my business at the American Embassy and go back to Chiangmai.

The following day was Tuesday, and Phorn was now well enough for us to go somewhere. I telephoned Mr. Robert Hasting, who was working as third secretary at the American Embassy and who knew me well through being married to a woman who was a student colleague of mine from Laos. I said to him that I was in Bangkok and did not have time to make an appointment before, but asked him to do it for me with the officer who was looking after marriage and immigration matters. He went away for a few minutes and said I could come in one hour.

Now I was not sure anymore why I wanted the information. Earlier, I had thought I would get it for Pafua, but now I did not know whether it was for Phorn, or maybe for no one, maybe just for myself. We went by taxi to the Embassy that was on Silom Road. Phorn wanted to be in her best, so the night before we went to buy her a nice suit that would not make her look like "someone from the street" as she said.

After I got the information I wanted and the necessary forms, I asked the receptionist if I could see Robert to thank him and to catch up on old times. After he came out of his office, we went down to the lobby area on the ground floor for a cup of coffee — the Embassy was on the tenth floor.

When Robert saw Phorn tagging along, he asked me, "Is this the woman you are going to marry? She doesn't look very young to me."

"Well, I don't know. She's a good friend. She just came along to have a look at this big, polluted city. She has not been here before," I explained.

"One of those country girls?" he asked, giving me a sneaky look.

"I suppose so."

"If you are serious about her, take my advice, my friend. They are nothing but trouble. I wouldn't go near them if I were you," he said.

It was good that we were talking in English. Phorn did not understand, but I was sure she would not take it lightly if she had known that we were discussing her in this unflattering manner. I was rather shocked by Robert's attitude, but he must have seen many unsavory cases of failed marriages between Thai bar girls and elderly American men before.

After we said goodbye to Robert, we caught a taxi to the Emerald Buddha Temple and walked through the complex with other tourists, mostly German and Japanese. There were hardly any Thai visitors, except for the people working there. Phorn was delighted looking at the long murals depicting villages and royal court life of the old days and other Buddhist folklore. We also took a lot of pictures of her, of me and of us together in various areas of the Temple. We were surprised to see the Emerald Buddha to be actually rather small, only about a foot in height. Phorn said that she thought it would be big like at least two meters high, judging from what you read about it, and I had to agree with her. I told Phorn that the Emerald Buddha originally came from Cambodia in the 15th Century A.D. when it was given as a gift to a Lao Prince who took it to Laos and built a special temple for it called the Emerald Temple (Wat Prakeo), which now still stands in Vientiane, the capital of Laos.

"How did it end up here in Bangkok, then?" Phorn asked.

"Well, history has it that it was taken to Thailand by Thai soldiers who looted the Emerald Temple when they invaded Vientiane late in the 19th Century. That's what Lao history says, but the Thai may see things differently," I explained.

"Is that so? How do you know so much?"

"I studied Lao history in high school, but I have also read many books."

"I really envy and admire you," she said with pride, swinging her small handbag with her right hand as we walked out into the street.

After the Temple and lunch in a small restaurant, I asked if she wanted to go to the Bangkok zoo, but she said that she hated zoos. She did not want to see nice animals kept in wired cages or in concrete enclosures. So we went instead to Wat Boluang Temple with its high exposed brick stupa from where we could see the expansive Chao Praya River with speed boats running up and down, making big ripples as they went past. I asked if she wanted to go into one of the boats that took tourists for a short cruise up the river, but she said she had never been in one and might get seasick. We ended up just sitting on the jetty, looking at the river and all the colorful passing boats.

Robert's words about girls like Phorn came back to me. It seemed people had opinions about her from any angle they saw her — especially in my company. The hotel clerks and porters, the stall keepers at the markets and now Robert seemed to think that she was "nothing but trouble." Or maybe I was just being sensitive? It was only yesterday when she was very sick in the hotel room that I felt so much for her and wanted to take care of her. But now Robert's comments seemed to have made my feelings fly away like a flock of swallows in a meadow startled by the flapping wings of a passing bird of prey. Was this what they called a reality check? I tried to dismiss these thoughts from my mind, and asked Phorn about her child.

"Yes, she's a lovely girl."

"Do you miss her?" I asked.

"Yes, all the time. At the beginning when she was only three, we were together when I first came to Chiangmai city to get away from the village gossip and to find work. But after months of looking and I could only find the job at the hotel, I had to send her back. I could barely make ends meet. I have to use half the money I earn to pay rent and buy food, and then try to save some to send home every month. Sometimes, I have nothing left."

"Yes, it must be hard," I said as a way of comforting her, not knowing what else to say.

At one point, she asked what I would do after I finished my work in Thailand. I told her that I would go back to America, then try to find a job.

"I am taking things easy, and face them one day at a time. I have no long-term plan," I said to her.

"What about love and family?"

"Well, they'll probably come later, I suppose?" I said, not wanting to give a longer reply.

"Well, good people eventually marry and make a life for themselves. You don't want to do it?"

"Eventually, but not now. Let's not talk about it now. We have other better things to do," I said, pulling her by the hand to get her up from the jetty.

I did not want to give her hope and to lead the conversation to us. I was afraid she might talk about our future together. I felt awkward thinking about it, as I still had Pafua to take care of. We went again to the main road where we took a taxi back to the hotel. Once in the hotel room, Phorn said that we should celebrate her recovery and the good time we had that day.

"How?"

"Change hotel! Let's go to a really expensive one with a disco and bar, and have the time of our lives there."

"OK, that's a good idea."

We left the modest Washington Hotel in crowded Saphankhuai and took a taxi to a five-star hotel at Siam Square overlooking the statue of King Rama. It cost 1,000 Baht a night, a very big sum in those days. The room was big, and had many pieces of furniture, with a big bathroom and a sitting room — all luxurious like the Lanna Hotel in Chiangmai where we first spent a night together.

The first thing Phorn did after the hotel boy put our luggage in the room and left with his tip, was to dash into the bathroom for a shower, leaving me to put away our luggage. After I finished, I went to join her but the bathroom door was locked. I knocked but she told me to be a good boy and to go away. I went to turn on the TV and waited for her. When she finished, she called out: "Your turn, now," and dashed out with a big towel wrapped around her small body. I took time in the shower, as we had a long sticky day sightseeing and riding in taxis along some of the most polluted streets in Bangkok. I felt all itchy and uncomfortable. When I came out, the TV was on really loud and Phorn was watching some Thai country music program. She was lying on the white sheet on the bed with the cover drawn back, but she had nothing on, except a mischievous smile on her face. She looked so seductive and innocent, as she motioned to me to join her. I did not have to be told twice, and jumped into the bed with her, groping her, kissing all my favorite places like a hungry man and making her giggle as usual like a child.

We went through the usual steps and movements of love dance, touching, kissing and cuddling. After a while, she indicated that she was ready and I went gently to work. In a few minutes, it was over for me while she still had not reached her peak. She stopped her movements and looked up at me from her position on the bed, as if caught by surprise.

"What's wrong?" she asked inquisitively.

"Nothing, just too excited by you."

"Not true. I know you could last a long time."

"That time with you in Chiangmai was special," I lied.

"And this is not special," she said, sounding hurt.

I told her that maybe it was just all the walking and the sightseeing we did during the day, and that I would recover soon and make up for my premature failure. She looked unhappy, making pouting lips at me as if to convey her displeasure. I did not know what to do or to say to make her happy again. I was disappointed that we had come to this expensive hotel to celebrate and I could not do the job that was expected of me. It was now her turn to console me.

"Don't worry. We will have other good times. Maybe it's the loud TV. Maybe it distracted you too much."

"Yes, maybe I need just you and me. But let's not talk about it anymore," I said to her, putting her small head with its short and soft hair on my chest as we sat on the bed, leaning against the headrest.

"You think we are good for each other?" she asked as if to make sure for herself.

"Yes, very good," I said, not only wanting to please her but also because it was true.

"You know, I have been so happy since I met you. You are very kind and loving, you never force yourself on anyone. I have never loved another person so much before," she continued, looking up at me with a sweet smile.

She seemed hesitant to refer directly to me, but I was grateful that she did not ask if I also loved her. Only her silent deep brown eyes seemed to be saying that they wanted me to feel the bright flames of her love for me, to draw me to them, to be consumed by them. I was uncertain about my commitment to Pafua, but I also did not want my relationship with Phorn to go beyond the point where we felt we could not live without each other, where I also had to declare my love for her.

"That time at the Lanna Hotel, do you remember?" she asked again.

"Yes, I do. Very well."

"That time, you asked me why I cried so loud when we were making love. I did not answer you then, because the time was not right. I want to tell you now that I cried because I was so happy. I just could not contain myself. It was as if I had kept these tears of happiness in me for so long that they just had to come out on their own," she explained.

At last, I understood her reaction, but I did not know what to say to her, for fear I might say the wrong thing, so I merely asked, "And now, are you very happy like that time?"

"Yes, very…," she replied, pushing her tiny body closer to me and putting one arm across my waist.

We stayed entwined like that in silence, savoring in happy thoughts for a long time. Despite my conflicting feelings about my relationship with her, Phorn really brought a sense of peace to my life. I felt happy, relaxed and carefree when I was with her. But I did not want to reflect too much on this, for fear that I might come to really love her. To make light our situation, I asked what was the meaning of her Thai name.

"Good wishes," she replied. "Phorn means strong, stable yet soft. Thiraphorn means constant and nice good wishes. And now you have to tell me what your name means."

"I don't know what it means, really," I teased her.

"I don't believe you. Don't you know what your own name means?" she teased me back.

"Well, sort of. But it's nothing unusual."

"You know so many things. Tell me, please. I really want to know," she was pleading, thrashing her small feet up and down against the bed sheet like a frustrated, little child.

"Well, my name does not have nice meaning like yours. Boys' names in Hmong only refer to very common things. Mua means to buy or to get, a very simple name with very ordinary meaning," I said.

"No, it is not ordinary. In Thai, Mua means to be absorbed, to enjoy, to be infatuated. And that really goes well with you and me."

"I don't see how."

"You enjoy being with me and you are infatuated with me, aren't you?" she teased.

"Well, yes, if you put it that way," I said, not knowing how else to resist her.

"Yes, and I like it that way, so I will keep calling you Mua."

Chapter 17

We stayed two more days at that expensive hotel, going to the Floating Market and visiting most of the famous tourist attractions in Bangkok, mostly temples. Phorn loved going to these temples, and she would pray and offer incense to the Buddha in some of them. I never knew what she was praying for, and did not ask. Sometimes, I just prayed with her to make her happy, but I am not really into religion and other abstract acts of the mind.

On the last day, I took Phorn to a big shopping complex at Dusit Thani, near the airport. It covered many floors and was one of those high-class commercial institutions like Macy's or Bloomingdale's you found in America. It carried goods of all kinds, but most of them very expensive. We just spent our time looking, and did not buy anything because Phorn said she would not let me buy her anything that cost more than 1,000 Baht. In the end, we came out and went into a jewelry shop where I bought her a gold neck chain. She was delighted, jumping and smiling like a child. We also bought an expensive Cabbage Patch doll for her daughter, as she said that she was going to visit her village after our return to Chiangmai. She still had not fully recovered from her cold, but was not as sick as on our first day in Bangkok.

We got on the bus with the same company we used on our way down, using our return tickets. There were not a lot of passengers on the way back from Bangkok to Chiangmai — probably too many bus companies competing for business. These long-journey buses also picked up passengers along their routes, so there were always some empty seats. When we arrived at Tak, half way through our journey, the bus stopped for people to take a break and have something to eat and drink at the local road house. We went to sit at one of the tables on the open deck where many other people were eating and drinking. Phorn said she did not want any food and was sipping on her Fanta orange soft drink, sitting opposite me and giving me her starry-eyed look now and then as if she was really happy in my company.

I was beginning to eat when I heard a man's voice calling my name out in Hmong from behind our table. I looked back and saw Yangva, one of the Hmong radio announcers at the Tribal Radio Station which was operated by the Thai government in Chiangmai. He was a tall man, with a ready smile, and I had been to see him on a number of occasions to record Hmong music which the station had a lot of.

We got up from our tables to shake hands by way of greetings — a custom the Hmong adopted from their French colonial masters. In the usual Hmong tradition, I asked him where he was going. He said he was on his way to Ban Vinai refugee camp in Loei to record some Hmong singing for his radio broadcasts. He often went to many parts of the country where he could find Hmong to do these recordings. He said there were many fine Hmong singers in the camp, and he also wanted to visit some relatives there.

Yangva was looking at Phorn who had by now come over. She was standing next to me, and was grabbing my arm to hold onto as if we were a young couple deeply in love and on our way to a honeymoon somewhere. I introduced her to him, and he said a few words of greetings in Thai to her. I felt rather embarrassed, so I just told him her name but did not say what she was to me, as I really did not want him to know too much about us — especially since he was going to Ban Vinai where Pafua and her family were. After a short conversation, he said his bus was about to move out and said goodbye to us. We also got on our bus, and continued our journey north.

As we were nearing Chiangmai city, Phorn was still asleep, leaning on my left shoulder as she had done most of the journey. I woke her up so we could get ready when the bus came to a stop. As we were getting off, she said that she would like me to come with her to visit her daughter in the village. I told her that I would think about it, but I really did not have much time because I had to get back to my extension work at Maewang. I had already missed nearly a week of work because of the trip to Bangkok. I was trying to put it as gently to her as possible, so she would not feel that I did not want to go with her to see her family.

I asked her to come to Samanh's house and stay there awhile before going to her student dormitory at the University. She was pleased with my invitation, and readily agreed. At the house, some of the visiting girls were excited and surprised that Phorn went all the way to Bangkok with me when most of them could only dream about it. They asked what we had bought, and Phorn showed off her new clothes and other things I had purchased for her. I apologized I did not buy anyone anything. Samanh was home, too, but he did not say anything much to Phorn or me, just looking on at us silently like a Godfather.

About an hour later, I went to see Phorn off when she was leaving for her dormitory. On the footpath as we were waiting for a taxi, she suddenly said as if to herself, "I don't have any money to get home."

"That's right. I am sorry I forgot," I said, taking out 500 Baht from my wallet and giving it to her.

"I wonder if I could borrow some money from you so I can go to the village to see my daughter," she said rather embarrassingly.

"How much do you need?" I asked, surprised that she needed more than what I already gave her.

"Ten thousand Baht," she said shyly.

That was a lot of money for a loan, but it was not beyond my means, although I knew that if I gave it to her, I might never get it back.

"I will check my bank balance tomorrow to see how much money I have. Come and see me tomorrow evening," I said.

The next day I got out 8,000 Baht from the bank, leaving me with just enough to cover my expenses for the month before the next installment of my exchange fellowship would be transferred from America. I had asked Phorn to come early in the evening, as I needed to pack to go to Maewang the following morning. When she came, we went into my room and I gave her the money. She gave me a big kiss on the cheek, thanking me profusely for helping her. At that point, Samanh walked in through the door — we did not close it, not wanting other people to suspect that we were playing some funny games in the room. He saw me give Phorn the money and asked what we were doing. I told him it was a loan. He then asked how much. I told him. He did not say anything, but just looked at Phorn as if she had done something terrible. Then, he left the room. She looked as if she did not know what to do.

"Just take it. It's my money. After all we have been through, that's the least I can do for you," I said to her.

She lingered on for a few more minutes, then said goodbye to the others, and we went to the street.

"You're so nice. I don't know how to thank you. I will pay you back before you return to America," she said as we were walking towards the road along the canal to wait for a taxi.

"It's none of my business, but what do you want the money for?" I asked.

"My mother wants to set up a shop in the village."

"Good. You will go back and help her?"

"Yes, if it does come about," she said.

"What about your university studies?"

"I will do them later, I suppose. I have my daughter to look after, and many other things to do."

"I hope you won't give them up," I said

"I hope so, too. When are you coming back from Maewang?"

"In five or six days," I replied, looking at her.

"In that case, I will see you when you come back."

Chapter 18

I thought I would be in Maewang for only five days, but there was a lot of work to do. Khun Surin, my Thai extension counterpart, was not happy that I spent so much time away rather than teaching him how to work among the Hmong villagers. It was another five weeks before I could get back to Chiangmai city. There was a letter for me from Pafua at the TDC where my mail was kept. She wrote that she was missing me and would like me to go and see her again, and that her mother also wanted to discuss something with me.

I was thinking that maybe they wanted me to propose again with her mother and to get the marriage over with, so they could decide which country to apply for resettlement finally. So far, I had only proposed to Pafua directly, but had not asked her mother or extended family for her hands. I had not mentioned marriage to them, but I assumed that they took it for granted that we would end up getting married and taking all members of the family with us to live in America.

After reading the letter, I decided to go to Ban Vinai for a few days, so early one morning I caught the Chiangmai-Khornkaen bus. I was anxious to see Pafua as soon as possible to find out what was in store for me, thinking that my wish to marry her would now be fulfilled. Again, I went to stay with Vang-yu, my cousin's husband, just as I did the first time I came to the camp with Samanh. It was about 11 o'clock in the morning when I arrived. After a wash and change of clothes, I went to call on Pafua but found no one at home. I had not told them of my arrival so I was not surprised. One of the neighbors told me that she had gone to Pakchom early that morning with some friends.

To make good use of my time, I went to pay my respect to the Thai camp commander, whose office was only a few buildings from Pafua's house. As soon as we got over the formal greetings and he asked me to sit down on one of the wooden arm chairs in his waiting room, he asked, "How are things going between you and Pafua?"

"Very well, I hope. I haven't seen her for nearly two months, but we write to each other regularly," I replied, knowing it was not really true.

"You should have seen her the last few weeks. She spent her time crying her heart out. I thought you two must have quarreled or something," he said, sounding very fatherly and concerned.

He seemed to know a lot about her, and I was alarmed upon hearing what he said. I was uneasy, not knowing what the problem was.

"No, I didn't know anything. She did not write me about any problems, and we haven't quarreled," I replied.

"Well, you have a lot of respect from your people. I hope you will do what is right. Go and see her," he advised.

I told him that I had gone to see her earlier, but she was not home. I left him at his desk, after saying goodbye. I was really anxious to see Pafua and to find out what the matter was. I went to the market and bought some fruit so I could bring her something. After I returned from the market, I found her home by herself. She was in the kitchen, trying to light the cooking fire — probably to prepare lunch for her family. I went in and sat on a low cane stool not far from her. She asked me when I got to the camp, if I had had anything to eat, and whether I had come after receiving her letter.

Having answered her questions, I asked how she was doing, and she said she was fine. It was rather hot, as always, and she had on a white shirt without sleeves and a wrap-around Lao dress — the dotted kind that women put on as casual dress when they were at home. She seemed to have lost weight, but did not look any worse than when I last saw her.

"Where is your mother?" I asked as a preliminary to what I was going to ask her about her "crying her heart out the last few weeks."

"She was home this morning, but I don't know where she could be now. My brother and sister are probably still at school," she replied.

"You know, as soon as I got here I came to see you but no one was home. I went to see the camp commander, and he told me something that really worries me. Is it true that you have been crying a lot recently?"

"Is that what he said to you?" she replied meekly, bending her head down and away from me.

"Yes, he said you had been crying your heart out. Could you tell me what is the problem?"

Instead of answering me, she just kept her head down and started to cry silently. I was never able to see people cry in front of me, particularly those I consider to be close to me. I started asking her not to cry, not to worry about anything and I would take care of her and get her to the US. We would get married and her mother would go to live with us together with her younger sister and her brother. As I was saying this, her crying became louder, and now she was blowing her nose with her right hand, and wiping her tears with the hem of her dress. She was still crouching near the fire she was trying to light in the kitchen. There was only smoke, but no flame from the firewood. She still did not say a word. Her crying kept getting louder, and now she sobbed openly, not even trying to muffle the sound or wiping away the tears. It was like a great release of something that had been building up inside her for a long time and that had to come out and there was nothing anyone could do to stop it. And she did not even try to stop it anymore. I now realized that my eyes were full of tears as well, tears that were rolling down my face onto the dirt floor of the kitchen. I kept saying to myself not to cry because I was a man who had to be strong, but my tears would not stop at the sight of this young woman who was crying as if she was suffering from some mortal wound to her body, to her heart, to her mind.

I moved over to her and drew her to the stool where I was sitting and we both sat on it, and I was surrounding her with my arms and was saying all these meaningless things in between my tears to try to comfort her. She just kept sobbing long strings of deep sobs that seemed to come from the depth of her soul — like some dreadful injury she would never recover from. I was wiping away her tears that were falling down onto her shirt. I was repeating to her all the promises I could think of, about marrying her, taking her away from the refugee camp and all kinds of other stupid thoughts that came to me. And I really meant them. I was wiping away her tears with my hand, wiping her face and her nose. I had forgotten all about using my handkerchief. She seemed so vulnerable, so touching and in so much need of protection and love at that instant. She still had not said anything. After what felt like an eternity, her crying and sobbing gradually subsided. I took out my handkerchief and wiped her face clean, and mine as well. I did not know when the fire she was trying to light had died. There was no smoke any more when our tears stopped. It seemed like the kitchen was cleared of smoke as our eyes were free of their tears, and a big burden had been lifted off our chests. We now could see our way more clearly, and felt much better about ourselves, about life, and there would be no more smoke, no more problems, no more sobbing and crying to hurt our eyes and burden our hearts.

I again asked her what made her cry so much, but she said that she was only missing me, and there were no other problems. I was really happy that at last she was showing real love for me and missing me to the point of crying and sobbing on my coming back from Chiangmai. Maybe, her tears were like those of a wife or lover after years of waiting for the return of her loved one? I was touched by the thought, and did not ask her any further questions. After some small chat about the progress of my work at Maewang, Pafua said she felt fine now and that I could go if I wanted to but should come back in the evening to talk to her mother. I thought that maybe she wanted to be alone, so I left her as she was starting the fire again to cook the mid-day meal. I asked her to tell her mother that I had arrived and would be back to see her as soon as I could.

Just as I was coming out of her house, I bumped into the UN regional representative and the Thai camp commander who were on their way to some official refugee business. The commander called me to go over and meet the UN representative, a young French national with some aristocratic name. We chatted for a few seconds in French and he gave me his business card. The commander was smiling, and I felt foolish with my eyes all red and swollen from the crying I had just done with Pafua. My voice was also hoarse and unsteady. They were nice to want to talk to me, but I felt rather undignified. I was not in the mood to discuss refugees with them and could not find anything much to talk to them about. Why does this have to happen at this time, I asked myself? My eyes were still smarting and I could not even see the UN officer properly. I was glad to end our brief conversation, eager to get away. Afterwards, I could not even remember what I had said to them as I made my way back to Vang-yu's house.

Chapter 19

Early that evening, I went to see Pafua and her mother again. They had just finished dinner, and Pafua was pouring me some pinkish boiled water to drink which was made from some tree bark said to be good for your health. It tasted a bit like Chinese jasmine tea. Her mother looked pleased to see me, but was very subdued with her greetings. I gave some money to Pafua's younger sister and brother to buy sweets for themselves at the market. Giggling and shy, they went out of the room.

Pafua's mother asked me whether I had heard from my mother in America, how I was doing in Chiangmai, who I was staying with and if I had made any new friends there. I gave her news about my mother, whose latest letter was full of praise for Minnesota where it was now summer and everything was alive and green after the long winter months of snow and bitter cold. I also told Pafua's mother that I was renting a room with the Thai friend who came with me to the camp during my first visit a few months ago, but that I was with the Hmong farmers at Maewang most of the time. I did not say anything about my recent trip to Bangkok, nor did I mention Phorn. After saying that she sympathized with my mother about the cold weather in Minnesota, Pafua's mother did not say anything further. If she knew anything else, she did not let it show on her face. She only sat there on a wooden stool, looking as if she was re-appraising me.

After this small conversation, I said to her, "Aunty, I would like to ask you if you would let me marry Pafua. I think I really like her and will take her with me to stay in Chiangmai once we are married. After we go back to the US, we will then sponsor you out as refugees to live with us. It's a great country, and the American government and many church groups are very helpful to Hmong refugees there."

I was too shy in front of her to say that I loved Pafua, although she was sitting right there as well. Her mother took some time to reply to me.

"I know you like Pafua, or else you would not keep coming to visit us. But I have carefully considered where we should go for resettlement. I am afraid the answer to your question would have to be no. We are going to Australia, but not America."

I was flabbergasted. I could hardly believe my ears. I had come all this way to marry her, and the answer now turned out to be "no." I became confused. After the money I gave to Pafua, the letters and the visits — was this what all my efforts had come to? Was it not her who wanted to go to America in the first place by sending me her photo and a letter with my mother only a few months ago to ask for my help? I had come in response to that cry for help, but they had refused me. What was going on? How could I find the real reason behind all this? What made them change their mind so soon about me?

I was ashamed for being rejected by her, as I saw myself to be a worthy prospective husband for Pafua. She was just sitting there in the kitchen which was lit by a single light bulb. She had not said a word but just sat on her stool, looking at the kitchen dirt floor with her downcast eyes and expressionless face, leaning against a wooden post like there was nothing she could do.

Pafua's mother continued.

"My brother in Australia has sent us all the necessary documents and we are only waiting for the Australian Embassy to tell us when to go. He had some problems trying to get us there before, but it seems everything is now fine," she said.

"But America is better, better social welfare for refugees, better housing and better employment. The weather is cold in Minnesota in winter. But in California, the weather is just like in Laos. Now I am in Minnesota, but we could move to Texas or California where it is warmer. In Australia, I heard there weren't a lot of jobs and most of the things they do there they copy from the Americans. Aunty, I promise I will take good care of you all. And Pafua's younger sister and brother will get a good education too," I was bubbling on, trying to convince her.

"As I said, we have made up our minds. We also prefer the weather in Australia where there is no snow like in America. Besides, I can't let Pafua go with you alone to America. She's the eldest in the family and I need her to go with us to be our main support. I am getting old, as you know, and I would not be able to learn English to get a job. My other two children are still too young to work."

"But I will work to support you after I go back to America. I will get a job. The US government will also help look after you and maybe Pafua could work as well," I said in desperation.

"Well, I hope you will understand. We really prefer to go to Australia. I am sorry that it has to be this way," she said, as if wanting to put an end to the discussion.

Was this the fate of rescuing knights in shining armors? More like villains in dirty rags, the way they were treating me. I could not accept this decision, this waste of my time and money, my feelings for her and my loss of face. Before, she said she had nowhere to go, but now they could go to Australia. Why? I had given up many things to come and try to help her get away from the refugee camp, including Damdouan, my Lao girlfriend in Washington D.C. I had stopped writing to her, because I thought it would be better if I concentrated on my relationship with Pafua. What happened between me and Phorn was only a chance event, something I could not control and that would not last, I was trying to say to myself. And now, this was what I was getting for all my efforts.

I turned to Pafua and asked, "What do you say? You should have a say. It's your life, too."

"What could I say that my mother has not said," she replied, never looking at me. Then, she added "You know I am their only support."

Again, Pafua showed only that deference to her mother and her family, nothing for herself was taken into consideration. Then, I remembered how much her mother loved her and would do all the right things for her, like the time when she fell into the river at Khek Noi and her mother insisted on a soul-calling ceremony for her. She was the oldest daughter, the one her mother could rely on for support. This must make her very special in her mother's heart. Was that the reason she was trying to be nice to her mother who had had a hard life, but not to herself and to me? She was just another dutiful daughter who would sacrifice her own happiness for the good of the family. Now I understood why she had cried so much earlier in the day when I could not help but cry with her. Her mother must have told her about this very important decision they had taken regarding her future without me. I felt like crying again. I felt like screaming, sobbing and shouting in despair. I knew there was no point in my staying on, so I asked them to think over what I had proposed and that I would be back tomorrow for an answer. I said goodbye and left without looking back at them. I was too embarrassed.

The following day I returned to Pafua's house, but she had gone to the market. Only her mother was home. I again broached yesterday's subject with her, and again the answer was the same — they were going to Australia and not the United States. I then went to the market trying to look for Pafua, but could not find her. I did not know what I would say to her, but I thought I had to see her and sort the situation out. I went again the next day to her house, but found it shut and there was no one home. The next day was the day I had to return to Chiangmai. I went back, spent and baffled, wondering whether I would see her again and how soon. On the bus, all kinds of thoughts were turning in my head. Why did they reject my proposal after having led me on, letting me see Pafua and accepting money from me? Was I not deserving of her person, of her love? Was she really needed to support her family? I could find no answers, but I kept wondering all along the return bus journey.

Chapter 20

As soon as I arrived in Chiangmai, I went to see Phorn. I wanted her to come with me to some hotel bar and get drunk, something I had not done for a long time. I was down in the dumps and wanted to stay there. I could not understand how depressed I was. Maybe I just could not face the refusal, the rejection? Perhaps, Pafua and her mother just needed me for my money? Maybe I saw myself as someone so good that no one should turn me down? With my crazy involvement with Phorn, I should have been glad that Pafua had refused me, but I was not. Instead of seeing this as an opportunity for me to get on with Phorn, I felt it to be a terrible blow, a betrayal of my love for Pafua. The white rescuing knight had had his shield smashed, his helmet split and his sword broken to pieces.

Phorn was happy to see me, but said she needed to change. I waited for her in the sitting room of her dormitory while she had a shower. In the taxi, I told her that tonight I was in her hands and that she could take me to any bar she liked. After we got to the bar on the other side of the old canal, she asked, "What's wrong with you today? You have just come back from Loei."

"Nothing wrong. Just want to enjoy myself," I said, moving closer to the chair where she was sitting and trying to sound happy.

"But you don't drink a lot normally," she protested.

"I want to tonight — with you," I said, putting my arm around her.

We stayed there for about two hours, and I had mainly whisky on the rocks and sometimes shandies as well. Phorn was just happy having shandies. We danced from time to time, but stayed at the table drinking most of the evening, and talked about everything and nothing. I never told her what the problem was, because she had never known about me and Pafua. By 11 o'clock, Phorn said I was too drunk to stay on and got a taxi. She asked me where I wanted to go, and I said to her place because I did not want to go back to make myself a nuisance at Samanh's house. She said we could not go to her student dormitory, because guests were not allowed at this time of night. I told her to get us to a hotel somewhere, anywhere.

I had only a hazy recollection of the taxi ride, and was not sure which hotel Phorn took me to. The next morning when she woke me up, it was about nine o'clock. I had a terrible headache — as if my skull was going to burst. She was already dressed, and had ordered some hot black coffee for us. There was a terrible smell of vomit in the room, and the carpet around the bed was wet in many places.

"You were very sick last night," she said. "You threw up everywhere."

"I am sorry. How did you put up with all this stench?" I asked.

"Well, what can I do, except to clean up and bear with it?"

"You are an angel. You are my angel and my refuge," I said, trying to tease her.

After the coffee, we returned to Samanh's house and Phorn left to go to her university lectures. I was feeling sicker and sicker as the day progressed. Now the pain had transferred from my head to my stomach, and I needed to go to the toilet more and more often. By evening, I could hardly leave the bed to attend to my frequent toilet needs. Samanh saw the state I was in, and decided to take me to the hospital. As he did not know any private clinics and had also just pawned his tricycle, we went by taxi to the main public hospital next to Chiangmai University which was only about two blocks from where we lived.

When we got there, they could not find me a bed. All the rooms were full, and there were even patients in all the corridors — on makeshift beds and trolleys. By then, I was feeling as if I was going to die. My life seemed to be floating away and my breathing seemed to get smaller and smaller by the second. I could hardly move and had to keep my eyes closed. I thought to myself that maybe it would be better this way, maybe if I really died all my suffering would be gone and I would be free. I did not think about all the hard times my parents had gone through to bring me up, to give me life and to sustain me. I had forgotten all their joy and expectations of seeing me go to America to pursue higher studies when I was one of only six students in the whole of Laos that year to pass the scholarship examination and was selected. No, I was only thinking about Pafua's rejection of me and the resulting embarrassment, and I wanted to die. I was at that moment no different from a dejected lover who wanted to commit suicide.

I was put on a trolley and as there were no drip holders to give me a drip, one of the nurses gave me a drip injection the size of a silicone tube. It went through the big vein in my left arm and made me really sore there. After the big injection, I could feel my life coming back as I could breathe better. I did not mind anymore being in the corridor with other patients who were poor and smelly like me. I was just grateful that I was alive and not dead. I thought it was funny that earlier I did not care if I died, but when it was about to happen I did not want to. I was relieved that they had rescued me.

Samanh's wife brought me a blanket and put it on me. They left me in the over-crowded hospital corridor all night long. The next day, the head doctor came to do his inspection round. Upon learning that I was from the US and not a local, he said I should go home as I was well enough now. Phorn came in the afternoon to get me, and we went back to Samanh's house. I had wanted to forget my problems with drinks, but they nearly killed me. I was not a hero from the movies after all. I was just grateful that I did not die.

After Phorn had helped me get into bed, I felt really touched by her devotion and care.

"I wanted to take up your invitation to go and see your daughter," I said to her.

"Really? When can we go?" she asked, all eager and smiling.

"When I get back from Maewang. I'll tell you when that will be."

She took out her purse and showed a small photo of the child. Phorn told me proudly that her name was "Nauknoi" (Little Bird), but liked to be called "Noi" (Little One). She was about five, and looked a lot like her mother, except for the eyes which were rounder. Her nose was also bigger while Phorn's was slender.

"What happened to her father?"

"He took off somewhere after our divorce. I told you about this when we were in Bangkok. He went to school with me and we got married after we finished school. But we were too young. He would not find a job. After Noi's birth, he started running around with other girls and we fought all the time. But let's not talk about the past when we have the future in front of us. After you fall, you have to get up, you can't just stay down on the ground or people will step on you. You have to gather up courage and move on, even though you may be embarrassed temporarily or may have been hurt by your fall," she explained, her voice tinged with a touch of sadness but also full of hope.

I was impressed. I did not know Phorn could say something so profound like that. She was talking about herself, but it was as if she was also doing it for me, for my state of body and mind at that moment. Yes, she was so right — I had to get up and move on with my life. I could not go on staying down in the dumps, just because something had happened between me and Pafua. What would people say if they learned that I, one of the few educated Hmong young men, could not cope with some personal problems and had to get drunk until I became sick and nearly died? I felt rather ashamed of what I did, and resolved that it would not happen again, that I would take a more mature approach to deal with unpleasant incidents in my life in the future.

It was Saturday the next day, and Phorn stayed with me to take care of my needs. We were chatting and reading in my room at Samanh's house, and did not go anywhere. I wanted to rest so I could get better to catch up with my work at Maewang. Phorn went to get us some food from the street stalls in the evening, but did not spend the night with me and left after we had had dinner. I was happy that she had taken such good care of me.

I had another three weeks at Maewang village measuring the amount of opium fields being cultivated by the villagers and counting the number of coffee trees they had planted in the last three years to see what else the UN project would have to do to make any effect on their economy. I soon ran out of food so I returned to Chiangmai. After buying all the necessary supplies for the next month, I went to see Phorn so we could go and visit her daughter for one day. She looked ravishing in a light blue evening dress. We went out to dinner at the evening bazaar, near the old Sri Tokyo Hotel along Sourivongs Road. We decided to meet at the Sanpatong bus stop in Pratu Chiangmai early the next day. We returned to Samanh's house about nine o'clock that night and Phorn left soon afterwards to get ready for tomorrow's trip.

We met at the bus stop, as arranged. The bus left at eight o'clock in the morning and we arrived one hour later at Sanpatong, an Ampher or district town west of Chiangmai city. The bus was old and slow, stopping everywhere to pick up passengers. They just piled up their belongings on the roof, on the floor and sat wherever they could find a seat or an empty spot. That was how the transport system operated in Thailand, but it was better than having to walk. From Sanpatong, we had to take a taxi to get to Phorn's village which was about half an hour drive from the main road. The village was in the middle of rice fields and was surrounded by high bamboo cloves that made most of the houses invisible from the outside. There were about 30 families living there, some in small thatched huts, others in large timber houses with iron roofing. In the village, buffaloes, dogs, chickens and ducks were wandering around, and children were playing in front of some of the houses. In the middle of the village was the temple, a medium-size structure built in concrete and timber with the usual steep and yellow-colored roof.

Phorn's house was located at the southern end of the village. We had to walk there from the entrance of the village. People were looking on at us, curious to know who we were. The house had a timber floor on stilts like all Thai village houses, but was covered in grass that was showing sign of weathering. We were greeted by her mother who was sitting on a platform attached to the house which served as the kitchen area. In contrast to Phorn whose skin was very fair, her mother was a dark woman, taller than Phorn but small and frail-looking like her. She was obviously used to working under the hot sun in the open fields like most Thai peasants. She was living with her married son who, she said, was away on business with his wife at Mae Hongson, near the Burmese border. Only Phorn's daughter and her brother's young son were there with her mother.

I was introduced to them as Phorn's friend from America. Phorn's mother could not accept the fact that I was from the US, but was not a Farang. The children had a great time looking at the toys and sweets that we had brought for them. After some chat with Phorn's mother who was a very talkative and friendly woman, we went to explore the village and the rice fields that were green and undulating in the breeze as far as the eye could see, broken by lines of trees and more bamboo cloves in the distance. We took photos of ourselves, the village and the fields, then returned home.

I could see that Noi did not like me at all. She would come and lean on my back as I sat on the floor, but she would not hesitate to pull on my hair or pinch me hard on the shoulders. And it was not like she wanted to play with me, but more like she was trying to give me pain, like she was saying that she did not want me there. Phorn scolded her and she ran away to her grandmother but kept looking at me as if I was an unwanted intruder, a stranger who should never have come to the house.

Before returning to Chiangmai the next morning, Phorn took me to the temple to take some photos and we went inside. It had a big statue of the Buddha at one end of the temple hall, with smaller ones in front or on the side. A few people were there, crouching on the floor and paying their homage to the Buddha with their hands joined in front of them. Incense sticks and candles were burning on the raised altar in front of all the Buddha images.

Phorn got two incense sticks from the altar and lit them. She gave me one, and asked me to kneel down like the other worshippers on the floor, close my eyes and "make a wish." I thought this was too corny, like in the Thai movies where the heroine and the man of her choice always seemed to end up in a temple wishing for eternal love for each other. I did not know what to wish. I seemed to have a mental block. There were many things I would like to wish for, but at that moment nothing came to my mind. I just sat there with my eyes closed and thought about peace and prosperity for the world, then I thought about Pafua. I spent the next few seconds wishing her well on her way to Australia and I hoped she would be happy and find a new life for herself and her family, and maybe she would not forget me.

When I finished, I opened my eyes to see Phorn still deep in her thoughts with eyes closed and concentrating on whatever she was wishing for in her silence. After she came out of her wishing trance, we left for the main road. It took some walking along the small dirt road from the village before we could find a taxi, but we were happy running after each other having a good time and getting dust on our clothes in the process.

On the bus on the way back to Chiangmai, I asked Phorn what was it that she was wishing for in the village temple. She said it was a secret. She then asked me the same question, and I said I would not tell because she did not tell me hers.

She then said, "OK, I was wishing I could go to a beautiful place in my dream with a nice, good-looking man who will look after me and make me happy forever."

"That's nice. I wished the same thing, but about a beautiful woman," I lied.

"Really? Who's that woman?" she asked, eager to know.

"I can't tell. It's personal."

"That's not fair. You're teasing me," she protested.

"True! I'll tell you when we get to Chiangmai," I said.

"You promise?"

"Yes, promise. I'll tell you all about it."

But afterwards, we had many things to do, so I did not remember to tell her about my wish in the temple and she also did not raise the subject again.

Chapter 21

The next afternoon, I returned to Maewang to continue my work there helping to convince the Hmong villagers to give up growing opium and to adopt other cash crops. There was a lot to do, and I wanted to finish early so I could return home to America. I was feeling generally despondent and did not want to stay on in Thailand for much longer than I had to. I had asked Phorn to come with me to visit the Hmong village but she said she was too busy with her work and studies. She also did not like the cold weather of the highlands where the Hmong lived, she added. I did not push the issue further with her. I was not sure whether she did not like the cold highland weather or she did not want to be among the Hmong — like many lowland people who thought of hill tribe people as dirty and smelly, never washing themselves.

I went back to Chiangmai city a few weeks later to take a break from my extension work and spend the weekend there with Phorn. I had missed her company and wanted to see her. I wanted to be alone with her so I went to a hotel on the western end of the city near Pratu Chiangmai and not far from the bus stop to Sanpatong and Chomtong — from where you could continue on to Maewang. The hotel was only small with two-stories, but the room was adequate and cheap. It was called the 555 Hotel.

After a shower, I went to collect my mail from the Tribal Development Center. There was a small parcel from Pafua. It contained a letter and a cassette of Thai songs by Swanee Bhodhitep. The letter was short, not fully one page. It said that she was about to go to Australia with her family, and gave a date for their departure by air from Bangkok. She did not say which flight or what airline. She probably did not know, or maybe it was no longer important. I would not be able to go and see her off in any case. I also wished to forget what she had done to me, the suffering she had caused. She also said that she wanted me to keep the cassette as a way to remember her whenever I heard the songs on it. She would like me to listen to a particular song called *"Namta Rue Ja Kae Panha Huajai"* (Tears Cannot Solve the Heart's Problems). As I later listened to the song, it reminded me of Pafua and of her tears and sobbing in her smoky kitchen, which still echoed in my mind. It also made me hope that maybe she had more courage than me and had overcome those tears during the past few months, otherwise she would not have sent me this song. After all, tears had to be followed by better things in life as we tried to face it, however difficult that might be.

After I read Pafua's letter, I went to get Phorn at her dormitory nearby, but she was not in. I left her a note to say where I was staying and for her to come there in the evening. I then went back to do some reading in the TDC's library. The librarian asked if I was going to do another visit to Ban Vinai. I told her that I would not be going for a while, because I wanted to concentrate on my work at Maewang. I did not tell her about the problem between Pafua and me. I had not told anybody about us. Sitting in the library, I decided to write the last time to Pafua. In return for Pafua's small gift to me, I sent her a long letter to tell her how hurt I was by her decision not to marry me, and also to wish her a safe journey and a happy, new life. Two months after I last saw her, now that I could think clearly, it was easier for me to write down all my pain.

Before posting the letter, I went to buy a cassette of songs by Toon Tongchai, one of my favorite male Thai singers, to send with it. As she asked of me, I asked her to listen to a special song called *"A Man's Tears"* that said:

> One man's tears flow freely when all is gone,
> His love forever lost, his heart forever undone.
> Who will know when the bitter tears that flow
> Are more than the rains from Heaven above?
>
> Love is the spur and the breath that lead me on
> To do all things good, to face all my woes
> With eagerness, and to give with generosity.
> All this was done for love, yet love has no pity.

Hearing love's parting music with its last dance
Is like a nail going into the wound in the heart
Casting love's final blessing and a last glance.
Is that what love begets, all but suffering and hurt?

Love when love is not returned rankles the soul,
Giving it wings to wander looking for paradise gone.
Yet I regret not what I have done for love spoilt;
Sad and wiser I change but I did it all for love alone.

I knew that Pafua sent me a positive song to advise me not to use tears to solve the heart's problems, but all I could find for her was one which said that tears were appropriate to express these problems. Did I regret so much the experience with her that I had become bitter? Was she a more loving and positive person than I knew? I sent the parcel, but did not expect anything in return from her, as she was probably too busy getting ready for her journey to Australia.

I got back to the hotel about five o'clock in the afternoon. I noticed that the air-conditioner in my room was on, but I thought that maybe I had forgotten to switch it off. It was only a wall unit. I was feeling hot and went straight to have a shower. When I came out, Phorn was in bed under the blanket with her usual mischievous smile on her lovely face. She did not say anything, just lying there and smiling at me as I was finishing drying myself. Jumping on her, I let my hands roam all over her body and rest on the softness of her bosom. I was kissing her and squeezing her with my hands and she was giggling with delight. Afterwards, as we were lying in bed relishing the soft touch of each other's body, I asked her how she got into the room. She told me that she had asked the clerk at the reception desk to open the door for her, saying that she was my friend. I did not know that this was allowed in Thailand. She must have been very persuasive and charming to him for this to have happened. She said she had been waiting for me a while before I returned.

"Is that why the air-conditioning was on?"

"Yes, he turned it on for me."

"How come I did not see you when I came in?"

"I was hiding in the cupboard," she said, again smiling mischievously and looking at the wall opposite our hotel bed.

"You little devil, always coming up with funny ideas," I commented.

I was touching her face gently with my right hand, looking at her in the eyes, and wondering what I would do without this woman with her very white skin and tiny frame — this twenty -something woman who still liked to play hide and seek games.

"You know, I feel as if we are bound to each other," I said. "We have been through a lot together. You were very sick in Bangkok and I was taking care of you. I was near death after my last visit to Ban Vinai, and you were there to help bring me back to life."

"Yes, maybe it's destiny," she said softly, still lying on her back on the bed and looking at the white ceiling of the hotel room with its naked light bulb dangling under a black cover plate.

"We did not know each other ten months ago, but now it's like you have been with me for many years. I will remember our time together and I will always love you," she went on.

"Me, too. Nothing will come to separate us. I hope we will be together for always. You have been through a lot of suffering, and I want to make you happy. I want to love you and to give you what you have been missing all these years."

"You are so nice," she said, turning towards me, rubbing her tiny hands on my cheeks and on my hair.

"You are not just being nice to please me?" she asked as if she had been betrayed too many times before and could never trust anything a man said to her.

"No, I really mean what I say," I replied, cupping her sad little face in my hands.

"I am so happy. I will be good to you. Don't make me suffer. Be nice to me. If you hurt me, I will die. I will not be able to stand it," she said, her voice strangling with emotions.

"I will take care of you. I love you and I won't hurt you," I promised her.

I was wondering if I should tell Phorn about Pafua and the deep hurt she had caused me. I wanted to tell Phorn, so she would know that I too had had my share of suffering. But I decided against it, as it might hurt her to know there was another woman in my life since I came to Thailand. I also did not want to burden her with any more of my problems. Later as we were dining at a food stall in the Pratu Chiangmai market, Phorn said that she wanted to go back and visit Noi, her daughter, because she had been difficult lately. I told her that I wanted to go, too, as this would give me the chance to improve my relationship with Noi who did not like me very much on our first meeting a few months ago. We agreed to go first thing the next morning, as I was anxious to return to work at Maewang.

After dinner, Phorn left and I returned to the hotel.

I got up early the following day, had a quick breakfast and took a taxi to the Sanpatong bus stop. I was sitting on a concrete bench, waiting for Phorn with my hand luggage on the ground in front of me, and craning my neck looking out for her. I was watching closely every taxi setting down passengers. But there was no Phorn. I waited and waited until nine o'clock when the Sanpatong bus had already left. At half past nine, she still did not turn up. I was getting worried that she might have had an accident on the way from the dormitory, or she might have fallen sick. Maybe she had changed her mind and could not let me know, as neither of us had a telephone. I had to find out why she did not meet me as we had agreed the day before.

I took a taxi to Phorn's dormitory near the University. In the taxi, I was thinking that as Pafua had now abandoned me, I was going to continue my relationship with Phorn and maybe we could get married. I would try to get to know her mother and daughter better by visiting them with her. After all, we had great feelings for each other, and I had never known more intense pleasure with any other woman, except her. Unlike some who just let me do things to them, she always enjoyed and took part fully in our physical acts of love. She had taught me so much about what life could offer, never holding back — unlike Pafua who was always subdued and afraid to do the wrong things. But then, I had never really known Pafua the way I had known Phorn and it would not be fair to compare them too much. With Pafua, it was only the beginning of a relationship, a very correct relationship that could become great but so far, confined to just talking and having feelings — an emotional experience. With Phorn, it was very giving, very physical, but it also could become everything pushed beyond the limits of our emotions. I tried to justify the situation for myself.

At the dormitory, they went knocking on her door, but the door was locked and there was no answer. Her neighbor said that she had returned late last night and had gone out very early that morning. I asked her what time that could have been and she said it must be about six o'clock. I went to knock on the door, but all was quiet inside her room. I was at a loss as to where she could have gone so early without meeting me. I did not know what to do, whether to go to the police or go to Samanh's house. I decided on the latter, as Samanh might know something. I hailed a taxi and when I arrived, he was standing in front of the house as if he was waiting for me. He asked what I was doing there, and I told him that I had come down from Maewang yesterday and arranged to meet Phorn this morning at the bus stop as we could visit her daughter but she had not turned up as arranged.

"What could have happened?" he asked in his usual Godfather way.

"That's what I would like to know," I said.

We went inside the house and sat in the lounge room. He had a cynical smile on his face. He asked me whether I suspected anything. I told him that I did not know.

"You want to know what happened?" he asked wryly.

"Yes. You know what has happened?"

"I don't know. Why do you think I should know?" he was acting like it was a lot of fun for him when I was so worried.

"You must know something, with that smile on your face. Please, it's very important for me."

"Well, if you must know. Last night, she came by and had a chat with my wife. Before she left, I tried to tell her off you as nicely as I could," he said in a very casual voice.

That must have been after Phorn had left me at the 555 Hotel after our dinner. Samanh must know something more about her that I did not know. What could it have been? I really wanted to know what made him "tell her off," so I asked, "What did you tell her? Tell me more, will you?"

Samanh said that not long after I started to become friendly with Phorn, he had kept an eye on our relationship because he noticed that we were spending a lot of time together. That was not a problem, but when he saw me give her 8,000 Baht after our return from Bangkok, he became concerned.

"In Thai society, friends lend money to each other, don't they?" I asked rather impatiently.

"I think she has big dreams about you when you already have a Hmong girlfriend at Ban Vinai. I don't want both of you to have problems later."

"What exactly did you tell her about me?"

"I told her that she should not think of you as more than a friend, and that you had come to Thailand to marry a Hmong refugee girl you were visiting in Loei," he explained, looking somewhat uncomfortable for the first time as if he was interfering too much in my personal life.

"I can't imagine you actually said that to her. How do you know Phorn is after me?"

"Believe me, I know."

"And you think she is too low for me?" I asked, trying to sound as nice as I could.

"She is a poor country girl with a small daughter and an elderly mother to support. She tries hard to get an education, but it is not easy. She must think you are Heaven-sent. Haven't you seen the way she has been acting towards you? In Thailand, we have a saying that people have to be humble or *"jiam tua"* and know their place. You are like the moon, and she is like a rabbit pining to walk on it, looking at it but unable to reach up (*"katai mai chanh"*). This is often said about a man going after a woman of higher status, but it can apply to a woman doing the same too. When two people are so different, they cannot have a happy relationship. Anyway, I don't want you to have problems later. I have told her and put her back in her place. And you really have a Hmong girl in the refugee camp waiting for you," he said with a satisfied smile as if he had just done me the greatest service in his life.

"I know you want to protect us from being hurt, but I haven't told you that I no longer have a girlfriend at Ban Vinai. She has decided not to marry me and I have not been back there for some time," I said.

"I am sorry. I didn't know. Anyway, I still think that Phorn is not right for you," he added.

"What other reasons do you have to say that about her?" I asked, showing my increasing impatience.

"You are a young man. You may be either too naive or too blind, but you don't know much about her and some of the things she does."

"What things?"

He went on to explain that after he saw me give her 8,000 Baht, he became suspicious. He had her followed and discovered that she had wasted the money playing cards in her spare time.

"It's all a lie, this thing about her mother setting up a shop with your money," he added with a smug grin, showing his big white teeth against a tanned round face and short black hair.

"I don't believe it," I said.

"I am your friend. If you don't believe me, just ask her yourself. Or better still, go to the illegal gambling den down the road. I work with prostitutes, but that's fine because I don't have any education and can't find any other jobs. But you are not like me. You have very high education and a good position in society. People put you up there in a very special place. You have to try to stay there, and not to let them down. You can't do that with a wife like Phorn," he pointed out.

"What's wrong with Phorn? And who says I am going to marry her?"

"You may not want to marry her, but she does. I am sorry to have to tell you this, but she is a prostitute in case you haven't noticed. Why do you think she often comes to this house? All the girls who visit my wife are in the business. My wife is in the business. They just don't work here, but work evenings in hotels. Anyway, I have put her back in her place," he said with his usual grin.

Chapter 22

I was dumbfounded. I could not imagine that a man would let his wife work in this profession as if she was just going to a normal job and come back home when it was done. Although Samanh's wife had told me about some of these young women, it had never occurred to me that all of them were involved in prostitution, including Phorn. She had been my only friend and companion in times of misery as well as joy. We had shared many things and had feelings for each other that the so-called clean and good people would not have known. She was open and held nothing back from me. She had always shown great understanding and support, never asking for payments or rewards. She had a heart of gold. Perhaps, Samanh was just being mean to her, I tried to reason with myself.

"If she was a prostitute, she would have given me the clap," I tried to defend her.

"They all have regular medical checks. Few of them have diseases," Samanh went on.

"What about her university course? She always told me that she was a university student and nothing else," I said.

"You really think she is studying at the University? She did not even finish middle high school. How would they accept her into a university course? It's all a front. And the dormitory, it's only near the University, not inside it. It doesn't belong to the University," he said.

For the first time, I realized that Samanh had put some of the important missing pieces into the puzzle, missing pieces that I did not see before. Now that I came to think of it, she did force herself on me on many occasions. I had never been with her inside a lecture room at the University. She told me that she worked at some hotel to support herself, but I also had never seen this hotel or what kind of hotel work she was doing. She also seemed to know many hotels and the people working there, as if she often went to them, like those times when we went to the Lanna or the 555. She was also very experienced and carefree in bed and it now seemed that this had been the main thing she was good at, but maybe not only with me. And what about her daughter and mother in the country? How could she study and work to support them at the same time? She had never asked me for money, except for the big loan after our trip to Bangkok. Was it a loan, or was it a subtle and smart way to get a cumulative payment from me for the many times we spent together? I was afraid to know the answers.

"You shouldn't have told her off. Anyway, where is she now?" I asked, somewhat shame-facedly.

"I don't know. Probably licking her wounds somewhere with some rich Chinese businessman. Believe me, I am a pimp and a procurer, an old hand in the business. I know what most of these women are like. If they don't get into gambling, then they are into drugs. Few of them are any good."

I knew that Samanh meant well, but I was annoyed that he had told me all this now when it was him who first introduced me to Phorn. Whatever she was to him, I had never looked at her in any way other than as an equal human being. If Phorn had had the same chance as me, she would have done just as well.

"I was no better than her. My grandparents were just peasants, too. I have only been lucky to have parents who lived in the city and to get where I am," I said to Samanh.

"Yes, but now you are up there, and she is down here," he explained, pointing his finger at the ceiling when mentioning me, and to the floor at his feet referring to her.

"You shouldn't have told her about being in a lowly position. Now, I'll have to find her. I am not like what you say. I don't look down on people, you know me. If I did, I would not have come and stayed with you," I added.

"I am sorry to interfere but believe me, I am doing you a big favor. You will thank me for it in years to come."

After what Pafua did to me, it was then like a big part of me had died, for I had never been through such a rejection before. Now that I had lost Phorn, I felt like the other half of me had gone out to join the part that went with Pafua. I left my bag in the room and left the house. My heart was aching like it had just been broken to little pieces — by what and whom I was not sure and I did not care. I did not want to get drunk and become sick again, so I just went into the street and walked around and around, then ended up in a movie house. I could not make any sense of the movie. I could not concentrate. Samanh's words were ringing in my ears: "I am doing you a big favor. You'll thank me for it in years to come." Why did he think we would not be happy together, me and Phorn? How would he know when he had not been through all the joy and pain that I have been through with her? He would not understand.

Phorn had been the bright light of my life during most of my stay in Thailand. I had enjoyed being with her so much I had even come to love her. She was always there for me when I needed her. How could I go on without her? I had just told her yesterday at the 555 Hotel that I loved her, and promised to take care of her. We had not talked about marriage, but she had said that she would die if I ever hurt her. But I did not hurt her. It was someone else. Why must our relationship end this way when it was going so well? Is it true about those love stories where the lovers, after all the trepidation they go through in life, finally die and go to Heaven, not alone but together, to love again because their love was not fulfilled on Earth? Could this happen to us? Maybe the stories are all made up to make people feel less lonely, less despairing? I really wished I could know, but probably never would.

> Is love forever lasting, in life as in death?
> Or does it sometimes make us feel lonely instead?
> Are lovers guided by the kind fortune of destiny
> Or do they also feel lost in life's many mysteries?
>
> In times of joy, life is pink carnations and wine.
> But do we live it to the full in its moment divine,
> And then despair in the times of darkness and slight,
> Letting go of hope with no love to pass the night?
>
> Life is a rainbow, multi-colored and arching
> When the fine rain drizzles and the sun shines.
> Love is its colors, and hope makes it dazzling,
> But after the sunlight goes, where is the rainbow?

I started to really resent Samanh for the terrible hurt he must have given Phorn with his attempt to "put her back in her place," but I could also see that maybe he was right. Life was not meant to be smooth and straightforward the way we would like to see it. There were rules, there were things and people that society put in some pecking order and told you who you could be with and who you could not. We are not free to do what we want, when we want, or even to be what we want to be. We are forever at the mercy of society's clutches, of forces beyond our control, just like the way Phorn and I could not control our animal pleasure, a pleasure that knew no bounds. We thrived on each other like two desperate souls clinging together, drowning together and sharing moments of joy and despair with each other. We had enjoyed many other things, but we were best when we were fulfilling our physical needs, the one great thing we were good at. But this physical love could be the start of other great feelings, of real, all-encompassing love for each other. We had been taking what we could from each other, and savored each moment as if there was no tomorrow. But tomorrow always comes, and you have to be prepared to meet it, to accept the realities around you with courage and not to give up easily.

I wanted to see Phorn again to make sure for myself that she was not hurt by what Samanh had done to her, that she was not what he said she was, a shameless girl of the night who wanted to throw herself at me to get away from her difficult life. I went back to her dormitory a number of times that day to look for her, but no one knew where she had gone to. I became worried sick that she might have done something to hurt herself. She must have been very hurt inside, as well as feeling ashamed and never wanting to face me again. The next day, I went to her village in Sanpatong to ask her mother if she had any news of Phorn. True to Samanh's words, there was no shop set up at her house. I found Phorn's mother home by herself without her granddaughter, Noi, and the young son of Phorn's brother whom I met on my first visit.

I asked her if she had any recent news of Phorn, but she said that I should know better because we were both in Chiangmai and had more contact with each other. I told her that I was with Phorn until two days ago and we had arranged to visit them yesterday but Phorn failed to meet me at the bus stop. I said that I was very concerned about her, as I had looked for her everywhere yesterday but could not find her, and did not know where else to look so I had come to the village as my last hope. She continued to say that she did not know what could have happened to Phorn, but did not seem to be very worried like a mother should when her only daughter went missing. Something seemed to be amiss, so I asked her where were her niece and nephew. She told me that they had gone to join Phorn's brother and sister-in-law in Mae Hongson where they were now trading in teak furniture. I said to her that I really needed to see Phorn and to explain a misunderstanding. Before leaving, I asked her to ask Phorn to contact me as soon as she could if she came to the village in the next few days. I also gave her my address in America in case Phorn wanted to write to me later.

I was in a hurry to return to work at Maewang, and did not have more time to look for Phorn. I had already lost two days. From her village, I took a bus to Chomtong, then went up to Doi Sanpa with a Hmong couple I knew who had come to the market at Chomtong in their Toyota utility truck. After a few days at Maewang, I felt very despondent and could not stop thinking the worst about Phorn. While we were at the expensive hotel in Bangkok, she had said that she had been very happy being with me and that she had never loved anyone so much in her life. If that was the case, she must have been heartbroken being told to stay away from me. I only hoped that Samanh was right about her being a pushy woman, for she would then be more thick-skinned and not easily hurt. In the end, I was too busy to continue looking for her, as I needed to complete the rest of my extension work before returning to America in two months time. Samanh's many words of advice against my relationship with Phorn and her dubious line of work seemed to also slowly sink in me over the weeks that followed. I eventually stopped thinking about finding her. A few months after I got back to the US, she sent me a photo of herself with no letter and no address. At the back of the photo, she had scrawled in Thai "Don't forget to remember me" — with no signature and no date. But times changed, and gradually she faded from my memory like images in a photo album left exposed to the elements.

Chapter 23

A week before I left for the US, I went to Ban Vinai refugee camp to say goodbye to relatives and friends who were still there waiting to be accepted for resettlement in far-away Western countries. Again, I went by bus and followed the same route I had taken so many times before when I went to see Pafua earlier during the year. When we reached Chumpae, I went to stay in the only hotel there called the Queen Hotel run by a big, young man with the soft voice of a woman. The weather was very hot and I felt very sticky. After a shower, I went to eat in the market, then took a short walk to look at the shops but there was nothing much to see, so I decided to turn in. The next day when I arrived at Loei, it was late in the afternoon and the last bus for Ban Vinai had already left. I ended up spending the night there to wait for the early bus the following morning. I booked into a hotel near the main market, then went shopping to buy gifts for relatives and friends at the refugee camp.

After I returned, I looked out of the hotel window to the other side of the street. I realized that I was just a few buildings down from the old hotel where I took Pafua seven months before to wash and to change into the new clothes I had bought for her after we had arrived from Ban Vinai on our second visit to Loei. That was also where I first tried to show my affection for her by attempting to give her a kiss on the cheek but she wouldn't let me. Suddenly, I felt very sad and I did not know if it was because I was missing her or regretting my failure with her. Pafua's mother had refused to let me marry her, and I had tried all I could to change her mind but it was to no avail so it could not have been my fault. But here I was in this old, dusty hotel room by myself, and all I could do was think about Pafua and feel deeply depressed. I could not understand why I was feeling this way and wanted to cry.

The earliest bus going to Pak Chom via Ban Vinai refugee camp the next day left about nine in the morning. I got on it as early as I could, giving some of my luggage to the bus boy to put on the roof rack of the bus and dragging the rest of my shopping bags with me to my seat. It was not too dusty on the road this time of the year in November when some light rain still fell in Thailand, just enough to put down the dust but not too much to make the roads muddy. It was another two hours before we arrived at Ban Vinai where the first sight was again the large throng of Hmong refugees walking along the small road inside the camp perimeter just the way I saw them during my first trip. I felt the same thing I did then, a sense of wonder and shock at this large number of people, of all ages, living confined like prisoners in this very big, fenced-in compound surrounded by soldiers and barbed wire.

After clearing my papers with the guards at the gate, I again went to stay with Vang-yu's family. He had fewer children than my other cousin, Lychu, and thus had more room for visitors. After the initial greetings, my host and I started telling each other the latest news about ourselves, about our work and life in the refugee camp. I gave small gifts to women and children I was related to, to try and make everyone happy. My cousin, Vang-yu's wife, asked me whether I was still involved with "the Thai woman who broke Pafua's heart." I told her that I was not really serious about Phorn and that she did not break Pafua's heart, but the truth was that Pafua's mother would not let me marry her daughter. My cousin just said "is that right?" and did not say anything more on the subject, but what she said set me thinking for a while because I had never told anyone about Phorn up to that point in time. Maybe, some of them in the refugee camp knew earlier about me and Phorn than I had suspected. Or was there more to Pafua's decision not to marry me than what she and her mother told me? She put up so little protest against her mother at the time. Perhaps, she had only used her mother as an excuse, as a front for her own decision? Maybe, she did know about Phorn and had told my cousin about it since they sometimes visited each other? I tried to banish the thought from my mind, for all this was in the past. There was no use going back to something that had now disappeared.

I spent the next few days visiting relatives and friends in the camp, saying goodbye to those whom I might not see again as I would soon return to Chiangmai and then to America. On the last day of my stay, I received a visit from a young girl I had not seen before, but who said that her name was Shua and she was a close friend of Pafua's. Knowing that Pafua was no longer in the camp, I did not try to go near the building where she used to live. I was chatting with some relatives in Vang-yu's kitchen, and Shua did not want to come in. She asked me to go outside, explaining that she was the friend who was sick and could not go to Loei with me and Pafua so we ended up going there by ourselves on my second visit to the camp. Shua asked how things had been with me and I told her as much as I could in the few minutes we were together outside.

She then handed me a small plastic bag and said, "This is for you. From Pafua. She left it with me to give to you. I did not send it by post because I did not have your address and money to pay for it. I was hoping you would be coming here before your return to America. So I have kept it with me."

I was overcome with emotions I could not describe. I did not know whether it was fear of the past or happiness, or a mixture of both knowing that she did not feel bad about what had happened, and that she remembered me in spite of everything — with what was inside this little plastic bag.

"Thank you. Thank you for keeping it for me," I said in a trembling voice.

"That's all right. I hope you'll feel better about her with this gift," Shua said, as if she knew what was in the bag.

"Yes, I am sure. Thanks again."

Shua said that Pafua was still crying sometimes when she talked about me, even up to the time she left for Australia. She had not written back to give any forwarding address. Shua told me which building she lived in and asked me to visit her and her family if I needed to, then said goodbye and left. I returned to Vang-yu's kitchen where the other visitors were still waiting for me. I put the bag in a corner and we resumed conversation as before, although I felt rather distraught to hear about Pafua again. There were probably many things I did not know about her. Later in the afternoon I took a walk to the camp market to get some drink, taking Pafua's bag with me. After I had sat down at a small table in a noodle shop and ordered a glass of iced, black coffee, I put the bag on the table and pulled out its content which was carefully wrapped in brown paper sealed with clear, sticky tape. On one side of it was a pink envelop addressed to me in Pafua's small, Lao hand-writing that I knew so well.

I opened the letter. It did not have my name on it, but its message was clearly for me.

> *My dear one,*
>
> *Last night, they said the bus would be here at dawn tomorrow to take us to Bangkok where we would stay a few weeks for our health clearance and to wait for our papers to be processed by the Australian Embassy before we would get on the plane to go to Australia.*
>
> *I am so afraid that I will not have enough time to write you this letter and to give you my last parting gifts. I did not have time to send them to you by post because I had just finished working on the pillow cases. I will have to give them to Shua, my best friend, and ask her to pass them on to you. I hope when you get them you will like them for what they represent.*
>
> *I did all the embroidery on the pillow cases with my own hands. They are very dear to me and I want to give them to you, for you and whoever will be sharing your life, to remember me. When you lie down in bed and put your head on these silk pillow cases, I hope you will think of me and the times we had together. More than anything else, I hope that one day you will know why I have to go from you, even though I was the one who first asked you to come for me in Thailand. If I could I would have moved the world to be with you, but that was not to be. I am sorry about this sad turn of events for the two of us.*
>
> *At first, I was not going to leave you with any more things from me. You have got the cassette of my favorite Thai songs which I sent by post more than a month ago, and you have some of the photos that you took of me when we went to the public garden in Loei. But I changed my mind when you sent me your last*

letter with a cassette of Thai songs: the one called "A Man's Tears" was so sad it made me think a great deal about you. Then, Yangva came here from Chiangmai a few weeks ago, and he told my mother that after you returned from your last visit to me, you became very sick and nearly died in the hospital.

How did that happen, my dear one? When I learned about this, I was so worried I could not sleep. I hope you did not become sick because of me. If it is, then I hope you will feel better when you get this letter and these small gifts. Since I had not heard from you again, I did not have any news of you. Is anyone taking care of you? I wish I could see you again just to make sure that you are all right. You must take care of yourself, and do not worry too much about me or my family. We are fine, and I am sure everything will work out for us in Australia. I want you to remember that even if I cannot be with you in body, I will always be with you in spirit.

I am feeling so apprehensive about going. Leaving the old country and this refugee camp is like leaving my past and a big part of me behind, like I will never see them again. I suppose the problem is that we are going to a new place we have never been before and do not know what is waiting for us, to an unknown future, an unknown country.

It is now past midnight. They have turned off the electricity generator, and I am writing by the flickering candle light. The bus would be here in a few hours. Promise me you will take good care of yourself because I will not be able to do it for you. I will always remember and will forever be thankful for what you have done for me and my family. Please do not give up on life, try to do the best for yourself and other people as I will be doing the same.

I have also written a short poem for you in answer to the sad song you sent me. I hope you will like its positive message.

With fond memories and love,

Pafua

The letter was dated 26 August 1977. Behind the letter was a poem written on a pink sheet of paper bordered by drawings of flowers, the kind of stationery used by young people to write love letters to each other. It was carefully written, almost in printed form as if she had put all her heart into it, again in the Lao language like her letter. I looked at the poem and it read:

> *Time and life can but go forward*
> *Unable to turn back, we have to part*
> *Going our ways to separate worlds*
> *Making us shed tears of the heart*
>
> *Seasons and the time pass and change*
> *Nothing we do will they disarrange*
> *All we can do is hope that some day at last*
> *We will again love for all time passed*
>
> *Although today changes to yesterday*
> *Although with each other we cannot stay*
> *Have no regrets for I still love you true*
> *Never will anything separate me from you*
>
> *Our days can do nothing but go flying past*
> *Though you will always remain dear to me*
> *For all the years and for all eternity*
> *My true love for you will forever last*

I took time reading the letter and the poem, trying to make sense of them, to understand what they meant to say to me. I unwrapped the small parcel in front of me and took out two pillowcases with multi-colored Hmong embroideries on one side and cream silk material on the other.

On the way back from the market to Vang-yu's house, I passed the building where Pafua and her family used to live. I could not help going to look at the outside kitchen where we used to spend much time together and where she was crying on my last visit to her. It was now very bare. An old Hmong woman I did not know, was sitting next to the fireplace. I did not go inside, but just peered in. She saw me and asked who I was looking for. I told her that I used to know the people who lived there a few months before. She said that her family had just escaped a few days ago from Laos, following the recent crack-down of

Hmong resistance against the new Lao government by thousands of Vietnamese troops in the highlands of northern Laos. I asked how many of them escaped to Thailand with her, and she said nearly 2,000 people but only about half of them ever arrived. She did not know what happened to the others, but thought maybe they were killed by soldiers or gave up on the perilous journey and returned to their jungle hide-outs. Like many of the Hmong refugees in the camp, she said that she was hoping her family could go to the US for resettlement. I wished her all the best and left.

I left Ban Vinai early the next day for the last time. I took the bus back to Loei, and then changed to the Chumpae bus. I arrived at Chumpae about four in the afternoon, and again went to stay at the Queen Hotel. That night after dinner and in the safety of my hotel room, I took out Pafua's letter and pillow cases and looked at them — the small gifts from the Hmong girl I had come to Thailand to marry, but ended up without her. It was really puzzling that before she went, she left me these pillowcases, a love poem and a letter. What she wrote seemed to show a very nice and warm person I did not fully know. It was like she was saying that she did love me and worried a lot about me. She did not say anything like that when we were together. Maybe, she was not someone who could express feelings verbally, but she put them down very beautifully on paper.

I re-read the letter and the poem as if to help me understand again what she was trying to tell me. After I finished, I felt an utter sense of loss and was near tears, for although they appeared to be full of hope and were nicely worded, they were also very sad. Maybe, she really did love me in her own way? Women seemed to show their feelings in so many different guises. You have to be able to read the signs, the messages between the lines, as some of them do not like putting their feelings into words. I am a verbal person and prefer to say things rather than let others guess or interpret my body language. Isn't that what most Asians do, I asked myself? Body language is not used in many Asian cultures, and most Asian people keep their feelings and thinking to themselves. They believe it is undignified to have to spell things out openly. Was Pafua like this and I failed to read her true feelings for me?

Chapter 24

After returning to America, I was lucky to be able to get a job within a few weeks of searching. The work involved helping Indochinese refugees to set up market gardening as a way to make a living for those with farming backgrounds. It was a project recently initiated by one of the counties where a lot of Hmong had resettled. I later met and married a young Hmong girl in Wisconsin who was a most understanding and supportive life companion. I had never tried to hide anything about my past from her, and she knew all about Pafua. After a few years, we managed to save enough money to buy a big house in a nice neighborhood in the suburbs and had two lovely children. Life was as happy as I could hope for.

Last year, I went back to Chiangmai with my wife. We were trying to look for Samanh and his family, with whom I had lost touch since my return to America in 1978, but we could not find them. Everything had changed. The city had greatly expanded, almost joining to the nearby towns that were now linked by four-lane highways from east to west and the city surrounds. Many of the vacant lots that used to exist in various parts of Chiangmai were now all developed. The timber houses we used to know had been demolished and replaced by new, multi-story brick structures. None of the people living in them were known to us. Even the dormitory used by Phorn had been torn down. A new office block had been built in its place. It was now almost like a different city, a different time, and the past had become just a flickering collection of distant images, another country, not what we now saw in front of us.

Now and then, I thought of Pafua. I still could recall what she said in her poem and last letter which she asked Shua to give me on my last visit to Ban Vinai at the end of my stay in Thailand in 1977. I still had her Thai songs which I listened to from time to time during these many years. I often wondered how life in Australia had been treating her and her family. My wife sometimes asked if I missed Pafua and we would talk nicely about it. Her poem and last letter affected me greatly and often made me wonder whether I had done her some terrible injustice by not persisting harder with her and her mother, or even carried out the necessary Hmong marriage proposal ceremony when they told me that they needed her to go to Australia. No matter how I tried, I found it hard to reconcile the beautiful words she wrote for me with her decision not to marry me.

In 1996, one of my Hmong relatives in America went to visit Australia, took a photo of Pafua and her two sons, and showed it to me. They were sitting on a window ledge in some high-rise building in Sydney and the two young boys were clinging to her arms. They were about eight and ten years old. She was looking at the camera, but with a shadow in her eyes as if they were forever sad. She had married a Vietnamese refugee after arriving in Australia, because she was said not to like Hmong men anymore. I pretended that I was not interested in her photo. Nearly 20 years had passed since we last saw each other. I had tried hard to forget what happened to me at Ban Vinai in Thailand in 1977. The Hmong refugee camp was now no more, having been closed by the UN and the Thai government some time in 1992, with all the refugees dispersed in their different directions in the world-wide Hmong diaspora. Its throngs of residents and teeming life had now gone, and only some distant memories remained in people's minds.

A few years after I returned from Thailand, my interest in the settlement of Hmong asylum seekers increased. I started to write about them and became well-known for my writings. I was invited to a few other countries to do research on the Hmong or to deliver talks at international conferences. Last year, I went with my wife to a conference on Indochinese refugees in Melbourne, Victoria, in southeastern Australia. It would be the first time for us to visit this part of the world, and we would be seeing relatives and old friends who had taken up residence there as refugees from Laos. I teased my wife that as there were only less than 2,000 Hmong living in Australia, perhaps we might even come across Pafua and her family in Sydney. My wife said that I'd better leave the past alone and should not try to visit Pafua on purpose.

Her prominent uncle who lived in Meadow Heights, one of the new suburbs on the outskirts of Melbourne, gave a dinner in my honor, and everyone was there. All his daughters and their husbands, his nephews and nieces living in the area were at the gathering. We had a great time together catching up on the latest news about the Hmong people, now living in different corners of the world. But there was no Pafua at the party, nor did anyone even mention her at the dinner table. She had become a taboo subject, and I did not dare to ask about her. It was as if she had become too sensitive an issue, too much for everyone, or else too unimportant to even cross anyone's mind.

Later, we travelled down to Hobart, Tasmania, the southernmost state of Australia where a number of my cousins were living. We spent the night in the apartment of one of them. His name is Xaichu. Like most of the Hmong refugees, he used to be a military officer before 1975 in Laos. The next day he took me to the shopping center in the city to buy some postcards. As we were walking from a crowded square towards a small park surrounded by beautiful flower beds and a big sandstone gothic church, Xaichu asked me, "Since coming here, have you heard about Pafua at all?"

I was surprised that he knew about her and me. I asked him how he knew.

"Around here, most people know what happened between you and her. It was quite a famous story, even for the people in the refugee camp at the time."

"I didn't know. Tell me, what story have they told about us?" I asked, curious.

He said that although Pafua got married and was living in Sydney not long after they arrived in Australia, her mother used to live in Melbourne with her uncle for many years. She was getting old and was not able to find employment. Her younger daughter had gotten married too, and moved away. Only her young son was with her, but he was still going to school. She was subsisting on government welfare payments and it had taken her many years to pay back the money she borrowed from a relative in the refugee camp in 1977 to pay for Pafua's bail. This relative had also been living in another city in Australia, but had since passed away.

"What bail?" I asked, suddenly interested.

"You really did not know about this? No one had told you all these years?"

"No, I knew nothing about bail money for Pafua in 1977. What did she do, was she in jail?"

"So you really don't know?" my cousin continued as we sat down on a wooden bench in the park in downtown Hobart.

My cousin recounted that after meeting me at the Tak bus station, Yangva, the Hmong radio announcer, went on to Ban Vinai. He had heard that Pafua's mother had a good collection of Hmong folk songs, and had gone to visit her to see if he could duplicate some for his radio work. Knowing that he was from Chiangmai, Pafua's mother had asked if he knew me. Yangva did not know about my relationship with Pafua and told her mother that he had met me the day before with my Thai girlfriend and that we were on our way back to Chiangmai after spending a week sightseeing in Bangkok.

Pafua had heard what he said about the Thai girlfriend and the trip to Bangkok. Without her mother knowing, she and a female friend left Ban Vinai the next day to try to come to Chiangmai and confirm the story with me. They had been on the bus to Chumpae for almost half a day when the police boarded the bus to ask for passengers' identity papers — a routine they always carried out in those days. The two young refugee girls did not have any papers that allowed them to travel outside the refugee camp. They had decided to take a big risk and hoped for the best. They were taken off the bus and were locked up in the local police station. The police told them they would only be released if bail could be found — something like 60,000 Baht or more than 2,000 US dollars for both of them, a huge sum of money in 1977. The two girls were in the middle of nowhere — unable to contact relatives in the refugee camp or me. Pafua told the police that the trip was all her idea, and they could keep her locked in the police station but should let her friend go back to the camp to bring the money over to pay for their bail.

The police let her friend go, and Pafua remained at the station. Some time during the night, four new police officers came on duty. One of them took her to spend the night at his house and something happened. No one really knew what actually took place. When her mother and a male relative arrived to bail her out, they found her back at the police station but hysterical and detached from her surroundings. She was a very beautiful girl who would be easy prey to men, especially men who believed they held power in their hands. In a country like Thailand where some local authorities sometimes dictated their own law, anything could have happened. From then on, Pafua had not been the same, quiet and always keeping to herself.

"And that was why they decided to come to Australia rather than go with me to the US?" I asked my cousin.

"Yes. They think that like many Hmong men, you would not marry a girl who had been in that situation. Some Hmong men even divorce their wives after they have been the victims of such violation. Because of this, Pafua and her mother had tried to hide the incident from people for many years."

"And especially from me," I added.

"Yes. It took about five or six years after they arrived in Australia before Pafua's mother paid all the loan back. The six silver bars she borrowed."

"Yes, that was a lot of money," I said.

"I think Pafua regretted not marrying you. You are now well-known and respected, with a good, stable life. Pafua has never been able to find permanent work and only lives in a government apartment with her young family."

"I did ask her to marry me, but she refused," I said to my cousin, remembering back to the time when she was with me at the Pakchom restaurant, looking across the drying bed of the big Mekong River towards Laos. I did ask her then and well before that fateful night at the Chumpae police station. I still could recall that she wanted me to ask her mother because not everything was up to her, she had said. That had stopped me from persisting further with her.

Xaichu continued.

"But you know Hmong customs. A girl who values herself as good and proper will not just say 'yes' the first time a man asks her to marry.

She is supposed to say 'no,' so it will not look as if she is too eager to throw herself at him. She will get more respect from him that way, even if she does love him very much. He has to get his family elders to ask for her hand properly from her parents with a proper ceremony — not just him alone with her in some deserted place. Only girls with no respect for their parents would run away to marry their boyfriends," explained my cousin who was many years older and wiser than me, a real Hmong person who lived a real Hmong life in the jungles of Laos before coming to Australia.

"If she wanted a proper marriage proposal ceremony, why didn't she tell me?" I asked him, recalling her silent treatment of me at that time.

"Well, it's not up to the girl to tell you what to do. If she has to tell you, it will be like she is really after you. You should know the right thing to do and you do it. It's now water under the bridge, but you should have asked for help if you didn't know what to do then."

The words uttered by Lychu, my other cousin in the refugee camp long ago, now came back to me, his words that people were watching to see if I would do things right with Pafua and that he was ready to give me help any time if I ever needed it. After her refusal of my proposal to her at Pakchom, I should have gone to Lychu for help. Perhaps, I should have asked him more about what I should be careful with in my relationship with her. Had I done this, I would not have made the mistakes I did. Instead, I just let the opportunity go because I was not sensitive enough to the Hmong culture and did not fully understand what Lychu was talking about that evening at his house in 1977.

Now I could not say anything back to Xaichu, this cousin I was talking to in Hobart. I did not know what to say. I was trying to find something proper to tell him, but nothing came to me. My mind was full of feelings of shame and guilt, and it now seemed as if I did not hear or see my cousin anymore. I was staring at the flower beds in full bloom of purple and red colors in front of me in the shopping square of Hobart, but I did not see any flowers. My vision was blurring and things were swimming before me, because my eyes were beginning slowly to fill with tears. My cousin saw it, but I pretended that nothing was happening. It was as if my body was chained to the present in Hobart, but my mind was held in ransom by the past and transported by the strong unseen wings of time back to Thailand in 1977.

Looking across the park to some tall office buildings with their glass window panes darkened by the shadow of the afternoon sun, I was thinking to myself that if the past could be turned back and put together anew, things might have turned out differently for me and her. As you get on in years, what happened to your life seems to belong to a different history, another sphere. Events are wept away by the wind of the seasons so you can never return to them in person, except to think about them, to mull over in your waking hours. Most of these memories you forget, but others remain deep in the recesses of your mind so you will always remember these other histories in you. The white and yellow flowers of the chrysanthemum blossom, wither and drop season after season and year after year, but new flowers always bloom again in their place. Old leaves falling from tree branches are blown away by the wind, but new ones replenish the trees and renew their growth.

No one can stop the breeze and the fallen leaves that had been swept away as time goes through its course, spinning new days and the hours fly past into the dark of the nights. Yesterdays will never again come floating back once they are gone from your life. You can only look back and wonder how things could have been if the time was different, but you cannot do much to change them. All you can do is to remember the rushing of the hours, the beauty of the green grass and the lessons of youth, to make the most of the present and to live for the unseen future. Like the scent of flowers on the trees, love provides the essence and the continuity to life in our moments of darkness, but it may also give us lasting pain. As with most things in life, you only see its value afterwards when events have passed like morning fog that disappears into the morning air, revealing the beauty of nature around you more clearly. That was how it was for me as I recalled at that moment all that happened those many years ago in Thailand.

After Xaichu had told me about Pafua's ordeal in Chumpae, I fought hard to control my emotions and tears, not to let them out there in this public park in Hobart in front of so many people. I did not want to show myself this way in this very open area, only at some other time in some other more private place where no one could see, in some other world of my own. But all I could think at that moment was the terrible violation my cousin had told me that had been done to Pafua, and my mind was besieged by untold images of her horrendous suffering:

> What did you feel when they violated you in the night?
> Was it unexpected? Was it horror, shock and surprise?
> Were you asking for help? Did you resist in your plight?
> What did you feel after the darkness and the sunrise?

> Were you thinking it was you or me who caused your pain?
> You, the blossoming flower that was not ready for picking
> With your scent still encased in your beautiful white wings,
> How I feel for you, knowing how you suffered and in vain.

It had taken more than 20 years for the answer to the riddle to fall into place, for the mystery to be solved. It was now clear why her mother had chosen to go to Australia rather than the US. They also made sense to me now, the words of the camp commander: "she had been crying her heart out during the past few weeks … You should go and see her." He must have known about the terrible thing that happened to her, as he had to approve all permissions for refugees to travel outside the camp, and he knew when her mother had to go and get her from the Thai police at Chumpae. Many rapes and other ugly incidents happened to refugee women all the time. Her last letter to me also made sense now when she wrote "I hope that one day you will know why I have to go from you, even though I was the one who first asked you to come for me in Thailand." Despite going through such unspeakable pain, she was still thinking about me and concerned that I should look after myself, as she "would not be able to do it" for me.

Why did Pafua and her mother hide everything from me when I could have helped them out financially and in many other ways? I would have married her regardless, despite what happened to her. Then I remembered that I once told her something I considered to be a joke long ago when we went to Loei and booked into a hotel for her to change into new clothes because the ones she had on were all dusty from the open bus trip from Ban Vinai. I had said to her then that I would not do anything to her in the hotel because I wanted my future wife to remain pure and untainted until after her wedding. Was that the reason why she and her mother had chosen for her to go as far from me as possible after her experience with the Chumpae police?

I only said those words to cover our situation at the time, but she must have taken them seriously. She obviously believed that I would not love her or marry her after she was no longer a virgin. Maybe, she really did love me and did not want to tarnish my reputation. Like her father, who died in the line of duty before she was born, her happiness had died just as it was starting. Is that why she had such a sad look in the photo I saw of her and her two children in 1996? Love often works in mysterious ways and it is difficult to know everything. There are things you cannot see or talk about, that are better left unsaid, a mystery, because it is not possible to shed light with a single torch in the big, dark cave of our short, earthly existence.

Chapter 25

After the conference in Melbourne, my wife and I travelled on to Brisbane, Queensland, in northeastern Australia. We wanted to spend a few days sightseeing there. We were coming from Melbourne and had to change trains in Sydney. I did not tell my wife about what I had learned from my cousin in Hobart. I only said to her that maybe we should try to go and see Pafua and her family, but my wife cautioned that it would not be a good idea as her husband might not be pleased with my visit. I had been most uneasy, since learning about what happened to her at the police station in Chumpae and the huge bail money that took her mother six years to pay back after they had settled in Australia.

The story had greatly distressed me and made me feel very bad about myself, about what my relationship with Phorn had done to the life of a young Hmong girl whose dreams were shattered by this chain of events. The burden of love must have made Pafua accept her fate silently and without protest, just like Khalil Gibran wrote on love in his book *The Prophet*:

> *Love has no other desire but to fulfill itself.*
> *But if you love and needs must have desires,*
> *let these be your desires:*
> *To melt and be like a running brook*
> *that sings its melody to the night.*
> *To know the pain of too much tenderness.*
> *To be wounded by your own understanding of love;*
> *And to bleed willingly and joyfully.*

As we arrived at Central Station in Sydney to get on the inter-state train to Brisbane, I was thinking that here I was in the same city as her and yet we could not see each other. We were so near but never so far apart, as they say. The train was leaving Sydney and there was nothing I could do — nothing at all. My heart was aching, but all I could do was watch the buildings along the train track sweeping by. Eventually, the train passed the Sydney Harbour Bridge and the beautiful Opera House with its conical and world-famous domes to the east of the bridge as we went north. The Sydney skyline was soon disappearing into the distance and it seemed that she was disappearing with it — the way it happened the last time I saw her in Ban Vinai. Once more I just let it happen and did not do anything about it. I could not do anything — she was married and I also had my own family. We now lead separate lives in separate parts of the world, as her poem said. The wind of time had blown away the past, and there was nothing anyone could do to bring it back. Life goes on, and you must make the best of what you now have.

We went to stay in a hotel in the southern part of Brisbane city with its many new suburbs sprawling along a new, six-lane freeway. We chose this hotel because it was not far from where some Hmong refugee families were living so that we could pay them a visit. One night after coming back from a tour of the Gold Coast in southeast Queensland near the border with the state of New South Wales, my wife was sitting by the window in the hotel room looking down at the busy street below. It was raining and people were rushing up and down in the street with umbrellas over their heads. My wife was looking down at this crowd below, sitting by the hotel window. On the small radio cassette player on the bedside table, she was listening to a Hmong song by one of the new Hmong-American singers, a cassette given to her by relatives we had just visited in Hobart. The song had a beautiful, melodic tune put to modern music and it was saying in the Hmong language that even if time had passed and could not stop its course, there were always things that reminded the singer of her feelings for her lost love and time would not take these memories away, even if the lovers had gone their separate ways. I heard my wife listening to these lyrics and I was thinking how apt and fitting they were for me and Pafua, for the story of our all-too-brief relationship and its painful impact.

My wife was sitting and looking down out of the hotel window. I looked at her from the bed in this small hotel in Brisbane, and it was like I was seeing Pafua sitting by the window in the hotel room in Loei long ago in 1977 when I was putting my hands over her eyes and trying to have my first kiss with her. Then, I saw a young, 18 year-old girl, with many hopes and much modesty, not knowing what life held in store for her and not anticipating any evil that would later befall her and change the course of her life. I saw an expectant girl with courage and many dreams, dreams of escaping the dire poverty of a refugee life, dreams of going to America to live and take her long-suffering mother with her. But the hopes were suddenly cut short and swept to the distant land of time by what the hand of fate had done to me with Phorn. In an unpredictable and sometimes cruel world, life is controlled by the fickleness of chance — like grass bent under the fury of the passing wind, like eyes in the storm that become blinded by flying debris and, like the hot summer dust along dirt roads that cover up everything in its path and makes all beautiful things invisible.

That night, I could not go to sleep. I was tormented by what Xaichu, my cousin in Hobart, had told me. Not only was the course of Pafua's life changed because of what I did, but it affected her mother, too. It was difficult for her to save and repay the huge loan, yet she had done it as if the whole thing had nothing to do with me. They had borne their cross alone and they had not bothered me, because they were too proud or too ashamed and preferred that I was not to be bothered. Yet, this very noble act seemed to have the opposite effect on me as if they also did it to spite me, to keep me and to make me pay. They did not ask anything, but in their silence they also took everything. I had to pay and to go on doing it — with my feelings of guilt over the great moral sacrifice they made which I was now helpless to do anything about. They held my life in their hands, and I would stay at their mercy.

Later in the night, I was lying in bed beside my sleeping wife, looking at the street lights outside the Brisbane hotel. I was still thinking about Pafua and how things could have been. Then, it started to well up inside me — slowly at first but building quickly. It was soon overwhelming me, blocking my throat, and I felt like I was going to choke and die. I was lying next to my wife in this hotel bed, and she was soundly asleep. She was a lovely person, but tonight I could not let her hear me and I did not want her to see me in this state, in this situation. All the guilt, all the regrets in my tormented mind were bursting in my chest, fighting to get out, and I could not hold them back. They were coming out in great rushes with tears filling my eyes, big tears that grown men should not shed but could not stop and had to let flow freely and unashamedly. They were becoming like sheets of water cascading from the furious sky and my face was all wet like the earth was flooded by the monsoon rains pouring down without mercy on its terrains.

I went to the bathroom and sat on the toilet seat with my pillow. I buried my face in it to try to muffle the fury of my pent-up feelings. My body was retched by waves of sobs, the way Pafua had sobbed in her kitchen in the refugee camp long ago. Then we cried together, but now I was doing it alone without her and without anyone. I had a debt to pay that could not be paid, a debt that I would forever carry with me. I was struggling for breath, but I did not fight it anymore. I said to myself that this did not mean I was not acting like a man, I just had to let it out so that it would not strangle me. After a while, the tears slowly stopped their furious course and I felt better. I felt as if I was getting my life back, the way I felt at the Chiangmai public hospital in 1977 when I was going to die from alcohol poisoning but did not die after I thought that Pafua had rejected me and preferred to obey her mother.

Now after the crying, I felt like Pafua had yielded part of my life back and had not tried to hold it all in her tiny white hands whose softness I used to feel so long ago. I returned to bed, and my wife was still deep in her sleep — knowing nothing about the drama that had just finished unfolding in our hotel bathroom. My pillow was wet from all the crying. I put my head on it as I was lying on the bed next to my wife, and I felt lonely in my suffering because I alone had caused it — with what I did to Pafua. I could not help but think that maybe this was what life was all about for many of us and for much of the time. We go through life and enjoy our greatest moments in the warmth of other people's company, but suffer on our own and leave this world the way we come into it — alone with no one as companion.

I admire Pafua and her mother for their sacrifice. I ask this girl of my youth to forgive me. She has been scarred and the scars will stay with her, but I want her to know that I too bear a heavy burden I can share with no one. With time, all wounds heal but the marks they leave behind never go away: they stay to remind you of your mistakes, of the injuries you had inflicted in that split moment when you did not concentrate or forgot to pay attention. Like the chance meeting between me and Yangva on my way back from Bangkok with Phorn, like when Pafua did not think about what the Thai police would do as she took a blind bus ride from Ban Vinai to see me in Chiangmai without proper authorization. These scars, these life accidents are like the marks in you that you can show and talk to other people about, but you cannot share the pain with them. The pain is best kept inside you because you do not know how to tell it or if people would believe it. I, too, have been carrying my own wound for what happened to her, and her lonely, silent suffering has also given me lasting torment.

One of the great American writers, Ernest Hemingway, once said that if something in life hurt you, you should put it down on paper. This is what I have done in the hope that she would read it and come to know how things had also affected me. As a man getting on in years, I wanted to say goodbye to this ill-wind of my life, to atone myself and to live with some peace of mind. When you lose something in life, you can only do two things: you confront your loss to make the most of it and become stronger, or you run away from the problem and become weaker for it. You cannot just look on, you cannot stand by as if nothing has happened. Should I try to brave the rain to find the rainbow so my torment may end, or should I just look on from afar and let things be? Should I flaunt all conventions and visit Pafua or at least talk to her? Or should I just let sleeping dogs lie, as they say?

That night, I decided that maybe it would be better if I could talk to Pafua for a last time to see how our tragic encounter of so many years ago had affected her, or whether she did not care anymore now that she had her own life to get on with. Whatever the situation was, I needed to hear her explanation. I needed to tell her that no matter what happened to her, I did not lose my respect for her. In fact, her courage and sacrifice had made me value her all the more. I was the cause of her dreadful suffering and I should be the one bearing the shame. I wanted to tell her all this, and now would be my best chance to do it when I was still in Australia and she was only a city away. That would do her self-esteem and mine a lot of good. But it was now too late in the night and I could not do anything anymore.

For now, I wanted to ask her not to think that fate and my ignorance of her silent plight did not help to make things turn out the way we both would have wanted. I did not know how to look through the dust along the journey of life to unveil the beauty that was hidden underneath. I was content to let the wind blow more dust on top of that beauty that I could not see. I was blinded by the storm of darkness and the summer fire of my youth. I regret that I was not the white knight she had wanted me to be when she first sent me her photo with my mother to ask for my help, but a villain who had ruined her young body and spirit, her hopes and dreams. And from the depth of my soul, I seek her forgiving solace and understanding.

THE END